'You think sex will make it go away, Rosalie?'

Adam's eyes glittered with a ferocity of feeling as he continued, 'Is that why you came? Expecting to burn it off with a brief encounter?'

Rosalie could feel the heat of his body seeping into hers, arousing an acute awareness of the hard muscularity of his chest, his thighs, and the powerful aggression that demanded she surrender to it. She couldn't think.

'You couldn't be more wrong, thinking the wanting is only physical,' he fiercely asserted. 'But let's test it, shall we? See how forgettable I am for you?'

Dear Reader

Many years ago I was fascinated by the idea of a family of children adopted from different countries, rescued from various situations and brought into a circle of love from which they grew up into remarkable people. So I created the James family and began writing a series of stories about how each one of them found their partner in life.

I began with Tiffany Makana from Fiji in *Ride the Storm* (1992). The second was about Rebel, the English one, in *Dark Heritage* (also 1992). The third, *The Shining of Love*, featured Suzanne from Canada (1994).

My husband died soon after the writing of *The Shining of Love*, and I lost heart in this project, which had been very much shared with him. However, over the years I've received many letters from readers, asking for more stories about the James family. The most recent one of these asked specifically for me to tell the story of Rosalie from the Philippines.

So here she is. I hope you all enjoy reading about her journey towards love as much as I have enjoyed writing it.

Emma Darcy

THE BEDROOM SURRENDER

BY
EMMA DARCY

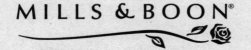

*First published in Great Britain 2003
Harlequin Mills & Boon Limited,
Eton House, 18-24 Paradise Road, Richmond, Surrey TW9 1SR*

© Emma Darcy 2003

ISBN 0 263 83331 3

*Set in Times Roman 10½ on 12 pt.
01-1103-39384*

*Printed and bound in Spain
by Litografia Rosés, S.A., Barcelona*

CHAPTER ONE

THE large group of local children surging into the foyer of the hotel caught Adam Cazell's attention first—something of a curiosity, given that this was the Raffles Hotel Le Royal, a mecca for wealthy tourists in Phnom Penh, and it was the cocktail hour. Adam paused on his way to the famous Elephant Bar to meet up with the rest of his party, amused by the chirpy excitement of the children, all dressed in long black pants and white tunics, regardless of gender.

Then he saw the woman who was shepherding them forward. *She* brought Adam to an absolute standstill, the sheer exquisite beauty of her catching the breath in his throat, punching his heart, wiping everything else from his mind.

Pale perfect skin, gleaming like pearl shell.

Long, liquid, shiny black hair, falling to below her waist.

Exotic eyes, black velvet, thickly fringed with long silky lashes, their almond shape tilting slightly up at the corners.

Finely arched brows that winged up at the ends, as well, accentuating the fine cast of her angled cheekbones.

A straight elegant nose, the slight flare of her nostrils balancing the lush sensuality of the sexiest mouth

Adam had ever seen, full pink-red lips, stunningly delineated by texture, not by cosmetic gloss. She wore no make-up that he could see.

A natural work of art.

Not Cambodian like the children.

She was tall, slender, innately graceful, and what country she called home, what mixture of genes had created her, Adam could not even begin to guess. All he knew was he'd never seen anyone like her. She had no peer amongst all the beautiful women who'd sought his acquaintance, and being one of the few billionaires in the prime of his life, he'd met legions of them.

With all his concentrated brain-power, he willed her to look at him.

She didn't.

She spoke to the children who gave her their rapt attention as though she were some goddess, commanding their reverent obeisance.

'Good heavens!' The surprised voice of his current companion, Tahlia Leaman, jangled in his ears as she hooked her arm around his. 'Fancy seeing Rosalie James here!'

He'd left Tahlia in the bathroom, blow-drying her long blond hair—a tedious activity that always tried his patience. He glanced quickly at her now to see if she was looking at the woman with the children.

No doubt about where her gaze was trained. She raised her other arm in a wave. 'Rosalie! Hi!'

The greeting evoked a frown, a quick look—the lustrous dark gaze skimming right past Adam—a rueful little smile, a nod of acknowledgment to Tahlia, and that was it, the briefest of interruptions to her communication with the children.

'Must be doing her children's charity thing,' Tahlia commented, hugging Adam's arm. 'Come on, darling. The others are probably already waiting for us in the bar.'

It piqued him, not to be at least *noticed* by the woman. In most company he stood out as a big man, well over six feet tall, broad-shouldered, powerful physique, with a face most women considered attractive, wearing well for its thirty-eight years. A good head of hair, too, though the dark brown was liberally streaked with grey, adding to his somewhat distinguished persona. He wasn't accustomed to being passed over by anyone!

'Who *is* Rosalie James?' he demanded of Tahlia, wanting some definitive tag on her.

It earned an incredulous look. 'You don't know?'

'I wouldn't ask if I knew,' he said tersely, wanting information not gushy nonsense.

Tahlia rolled her eyes. 'Only the queen of the catwalk for all the influential designers in Europe and the U.S.—the one model they all vie for to show off their star creations. The rest of us aren't even in the running if Rosalie James is available.'

'Is that a bitchy comment?'

Tahlia grimaced. 'The plain truth. I can't even be bitchy about her, though she does get the plum jobs. When she's not modelling, she works her butt off for orphaned kids and I suspect most of what she earns gets funnelled to them, too. You rarely ever see her on the social circuit. She's not into partying.' Tahlia slanted him a knowing look. 'Not your kind of woman, Adam.'

'No,' he agreed.

And they walked on to the bar.

But the image of Rosalie James lingered in his mind, indelibly printed there, a rarity that both annoyed and intrigued him. Why would such a beautiful woman spend all her leisure time do-gooding, not to mention pouring all she earned into it? What drove her?

Adam knew he was a born achiever. Building up successful businesses had always given him a buzz, though he grew bored with them once they were flying high. His latest challenge was getting a new airline off the ground and he was aiming to organise cheap flights to South-East Asia, scouting the possibilities while ostensibly on this pleasure trip.

To his mind, Cambodia had a lot to offer tourists. Here in Phnom Penh, the Royal Palace and the Silver Pagoda with its fabulous Buddhas—one encrusted with over nine thousand diamonds, another in Baccarat crystal—held so many unbelievable treasures, it was mind-boggling. And seeing Angkor Wat today—that amazing complex of temples built in the twelfth century—definitely one of the wonders of the world, well worth the trip.

He'd brought a few of his company executives and their women with him, and when he and Tahlia arrived in the Elephant Bar, they were there, still raving over what they'd seen at Angkor Wat. Adam left Tahlia with them and went to the bar to order drinks.

'A group of children entered the hotel just now,' he remarked to the barman. 'What are they doing here?'

'They've come to sing for the tour group having dinner around the swimming pool this evening. A raffle is being held out there, the proceeds to go to their orphanage. Their little concert is by way of a thank-you. Miss James organised it.'

'You know this Miss James?'

The barman nodded and smiled. 'The kids call her the angel. Sings like one, too. She does a lot of good here for the orphans.'

Adam frowned. *The angel*. He hadn't seen her as some kind of ethereal being. Her impact on him had been very physical. Sensual. Sexual. Which made it all the more frustrating that she hadn't been aware of his presence. No recognition of who he was, either. Not even when she had acknowledged Tahlia's call had she bothered to show any curiosity about her fellow model's escort.

What kind of woman didn't notice such things?

Most of the women he knew were like butterflies, instinctively seeking the sweet nectar of money. Like Tahlia, a top-line model herself, happy to be along for the ride for as long as it lasted. He wasn't particularly cynical about his wealth being a powerful drawcard, regarding it as the natural order of things. He enjoyed having the best-looking women in the world in his company, just as they enjoyed the high life he could provide.

It was something he took so much for granted that one more beautiful woman shouldn't have mattered one way or another. Except...being ignored had got under his skin, especially being ignored when he'd wanted to impress as strongly as he'd been impressed. A passing vexation, he told himself. Rosalie James lived on a different planet to the one he occupied. Pursuing her would be absurd. Non-productive. Clearly in her world, do-gooding had priority over... sinful pleasures.

He tried to block her out of his mind, chatting to his executives about the viability of establishing a Saturn Airline service to Cambodia. But when they moved from the bar to go to the dining room, he heard the singing begin. Her voice—it had to be hers—was delivering the verse of a very melodic song in a clear pure tone, perfect pitch...*angelic.*

None of the recording artists he'd signed for Saturn Records in years gone by had ever come close to having a voice like that. It sent a shiver down his spine. Rosalie James could have been a star in the music world. Still could. With her looks, her talent...

Then the children came in on the chorus, singing with more gusto than musicality, belting out their words at the top of their voices, almost drowning hers out.

Forget her, Adam savagely told himself.

He'd sold off the record company to fund the airline.

There was absolutely no profit in forcing an acquaintance with Rosalie James, either on a personal or business level.

Six months later Adam Cazell saw her again.

And was once more transfixed by her beauty.

He was at the Met in New York. It was the opening night of Puccini's Turandot. Adam was not a big fan of opera but he'd been hooked into attending this premiere—the proceeds to go to charity—by his latest lady, Sacha Rivken, who loved glittery theatrical events that promised lots of celebrities in the limelight. Their affair was new enough for it still to be a pleasure to indulge her.

Along with a festive party of jet-setting friends, they were seated in a corner box of the Grand Tier level of the famous Metropolitan Opera House, enjoying the buzzing atmosphere of a big night out. Sacha had positioned herself and Adam on the curve of the corner so she could more easily spot the most *watchable* people entering the two central boxes which directly faced the stage.

The far box was filled first. Sacha was speculating over who might occupy the adjoining box when the awaited party arrived and a jolt of recognition hit him.

Rosalie James...leading her companions into the front row of seats.

The liquid black hair was coiled around the top of her head, baring a long, pale, swanlike neck, around which hung a fabulous necklace of rubies and diamonds.

No sexless white tunic and black pants tonight. She wore a figure-hugging gown of dark red velvet—breasts, waist, hips, every feminine curve lovingly delineated to breathtaking effect. Little shoulder-cap sleeves swept into a low, heart-shaped neckline that revealed a tantalising hint of cleavage. Her carriage was regal. She looked regal. If she'd worn a tiara, she would have had people wondering what royal family had spawned her.

As she took the end seat, she smiled up at the man about to settle beside her—a big man, his physique every bit a match for Adam's, tall, powerfully built, his face showing a similar mature age, silver strands sprinkled through his chestnut hair, and he was smiling back at her as though they were sharing some very warm, intimate moment.

Never in his life had Adam experienced jealousy, yet a violent black wave of it instantly crashed through him. If her escort could have been mentally zapped into irretrievable atoms, it would have been done in those few out of control seconds. She had given *him* space in her life—a man of the same physical mould as himself—and Adam felt cheated, wronged, every muscle in his body clenching in aggressive anger at this trick of Fate.

'Oh! It's Rosalie James!' Sacha hissed exuberantly, delighted to have recognised the enigmatic top-line model. 'And she's wearing the show-stopper from this season's Bellavanti collection. I bet it's on loan for this premiere, getting more spotlight for the designer. And look at that necklace! On loan from Bergoff, for sure. Must be worth a fortune!'

Not money spent on herself then, Adam swiftly reasoned, nor gifts from a lover, which was a matter of some relief though he didn't stop to examine the cause of this relief. 'Who's the guy with her?' he grated out, wanting some firm identification, a name that could tell him more about her choice.

'Don't know. Quite a hunk, though. Very impressive.'

Which caused Adam's jaw to tighten further.

'James...is she related to the tenor who's making his debut here tonight?' the one opera buff in their party inquired.

Adam flicked open the glossy program he'd bought earlier. The starring tenor's name was Zuang Chi James. 'She's not Chinese,' he pointed out sardonically.

'You haven't read his bio, Adam,' came the faintly mocking reply. 'Zuang Chi was born in China but he was smuggled out to Australia by his family who wanted him to have the chance to develop his voice. He was officially adopted by a previous Australian ambassador to China and his wife, Edward and Hilary James. They found him teachers at the Sydney Conservatorium of Music where he won a scholarship to...'

'Hey! Rosalie James is an Australian, too,' Sacha chimed in excitedly. 'You could be right about a connection.'

Australian? Was that her nationality? Richard

stared at her, thinking there could be few more English names than Edward and Hilary, but Rosalie James didn't look English-Australian. And the guy with the reddish hair next to her looked more like a huge marauding Scot. Her slim, elegant hand was swallowed up in his as the lights dimmed.

Adam suffered through the first act of the opera which was utterly meaningless to him. He couldn't get his mind off Rosalie James and her escort, both of whom looked utterly enthralled by the action on the stage. She didn't once glance in the direction of his box, his seat. Every time Zuang Chi James sang, she leaned forward, her body finely tensed, her focus entirely on the tenor as though she did have some extra personal interest in his performance. Was he her adopted brother? He certainly won the most applause from her.

But it *was* his debut at the Met, surely a milestone in any operatic singer's career, and even Adam conceded he had a magnificent voice. Those facts alone could be eliciting her interest. After all, she sang like an angel herself, though without the resonant power of a trained classical singer. Finally, Adam remembered the proceeds from tonight's premiere were to go to a charity.

That was why Rosalie James was here.

Do-gooding.

Probably most of the people in her box were connected to the charity, directors of the board or committed fund-raisers. Except she was altogether too cosy with the big man beside her for Adam to dismiss

him as a charitable connection. The all too obvious
rapport between them was like a thorn in his side,
constantly irritating.

He was glad when the opera ended.

Supper at the Four Seasons was more his style.

Three months later their paths crossed again.

Unplanned.

Unexpected.

With the same stunning impact as before, but with
one big difference. This time Adam was not accompanied by a woman. And Rosalie James was on her
own.

It was a Sunday, midsummer in England. Adam left
his London residence, looking forward to the pleasure
of driving his Aston Martin into the country and collecting his daughter from Davenport Hall where she
had spent the first week of her school holidays with
her best friend, who happened to be the niece of the
Earl of Stanthorpe.

Adam's ex-wife was delighted with that connection
to the British upper class. Sending their daughter to
Roedean was pure status snobbery on Sarah's part—
a ridiculous reason in Adam's mind, but it wasn't a
big enough issue to argue over. Besides, Cate seemed
happy there, didn't complain about anything.

She'd just turned thirteen, his one and only child
from his one and only marriage, and a very bright
spark, indeed. He was proud of her, always enjoyed
her company when she spent time with him. They had
fun together, the kind of adventurous fun her mother

had never appreciated—going places, experiencing new things.

To Sarah, there was no place like England and she wasn't happy anywhere else, a fact she made plain by divorcing him three years after they were married. She didn't want to spend her life gallivanting around the world with him. She was now married to a member of parliament and was the perfect politician's wife, do-gooding with the best of them for public brownie points.

Adam wished her well. There was no acrimony between them. The divorce settlement had been more than generous and he still paid for whatever Sarah wanted for Cate. Money, he'd found, bought a lot of harmony. He could have their daughter with him whenever he wanted. Having made time off from business commitments for Cate's summer holidays, it somewhat niggled him that she had chosen to spend the first week of it with her best friend. Didn't she have enough of Celeste's company at school? Or was Davenport Hall a big attraction?

Having been invited there for lunch to meet Celeste's family before whisking Cate away, Adam took particular notice of the place when he arrived, driving slowly through the gateway and down a long avenue of massive trees, their branches intertwining overhead to form a sun-dappled tunnel. He had the eerie feeling of being drawn into some time warp.

Cate had told him the hall was over four hundred years old and the thickness of the tree trunks suggested they were of the same age, yet the leaves were a light pretty green showing a bright continuance of life. At the end of the avenue the driveway circled around a massive stone fountain, water splashing and tumbling in endless cascades, a sparkling pleasure. Beyond it stood an impressive mansion, three storeys high, much of its walls covered by ivy.

The impression of solidity and permanence was strong. This had been the home of the Earls of Stanthorpe for half a millennium. Adam had no need of deep roots himself, but he could feel its attraction here, the sense of security that undoubtedly came with nothing ever changing. Did this place have some special magic to it that appealed to Cate? Or was she being over-influenced by Sarah's values?

He was greeted at the front door by an old butler who'd probably served the family for decades. Having identified himself, Adam was ushered into a huge hallway, a wide strip of rich red carpet bisecting a floor of black and white tiles, a gallery of portraits on the walls, obviously depicting generations of earls. Adam instantly thought he wouldn't want to carry the weight of all this heritage on his shoulders, tying him to the one place for life.

Yet when he was shown into a drawing room of magnificent proportions and furnished with rich elegance, he could understand the tug of possessions that made their own seductive claim. There were three groupings of sofas and chairs and tables, one directly in front of a massive marble fireplace. But no fire was lit or needed. Sunshine streamed through a bank of six windows at one end of the room where a man and woman rose from another sitting area, smiling their welcome.

'Mr. Adam Cazell, m'lord,' the butler announced.

The Earl of Stanthorpe was tall and lean, but with none of the rather effete air Adam associated with aristocracy. He had dark intelligent eyes and a strong grip to his hand. 'Hugh Davenport,' he said, inviting informality. 'A pleasure to meet Cate's father. This is my wife, Rebel.'

Curious name for a lady of the establishment, and she was certainly a distinctive one—a mass of curly black hair tumbling to her shoulders, bright hazel eyes, an unusual angular jawline, a warm, winning smile of perfect white teeth.

Adam smiled back at her as he retrieved his hand from the Earl's and offered it to his hostess. 'How do you do?' A silly greeting, he'd always thought, but it seemed appropriate on this occasion.

'I trust you had a pleasant trip down from London, Mr. Cazell?'

'Adam.'

'Thank you.' Her smile widened to a grin. 'I've learned to be a bit cautious about jumping in with first names here in England. I'm from Australia and old habits die hard.'

Rather intriguing to find a dyed-in-the-wool English earl married to an Australian. Was he a *rebel*, too?

'Please join us,' she went on, gesturing to a nearby armchair. 'The children are out walking the dogs but they should be back any minute.'

She'd barely finished speaking when Cate burst into the room, throwing the double doors to it wide open. 'Hi, Dad! Saw your car coming up the drive,' she breathlessly informed.

Celeste was right on Cate's heels, along with a couple of Yorkshire terriers. 'We ran but you got here first, Mr. Cazell. Oh, do shut up, Fluffy and Buffy!' This to the dogs who were yapping at Adam—a stranger on their territory.

Two small boys raced in past the girls and the dogs, coming to an abrupt and rather shy halt at seeing Cate's father, eyeing him up and down before the older one—possibly all of five—commented with considerable awe, 'He's as big as Uncle Zachary, Mum.'

Rebel laughed at the remark.

Then in strolled Rosalie James.

She looked directly at him.

And all Adam's instincts transmitted a wild belief that the time warp in the tunnel of trees had been spiralling him towards this moment.

CHAPTER TWO

SO THIS was Adam Cazell…Cate's father…

As her nephew had just said, as big as Zachary Lee, but what of his heart? From listening to his daughter, Rosalie had formed the strong impression that Adam Cazell didn't give enough of it to Cate, whose discontent with her home life was all too evident. Celeste thought her best friend's father was *fabulous,* but that had more to do with her image of him as a daring billionaire businessman with enormous buying power.

A colourful man, Rosalie thought, if viewed from the perspective of his flamboyant achievements, but close up…

Then the big man's gaze locked onto hers, jolting her with an emanation of power that squeezed her heart and sent a weird shiver down her spine. Silver grey eyes…like bullets…tearing through defences she had raised a long, long time ago. She stared back at him, helpless to do anything else, feeling his aggression weakening every bone in her body.

Hugh rescued her, moving to draw the boys forward and introduce them. 'These are my sons, Geoffrey and Malcolm.'

It forced Adam Cazell to look at them and say something appropriate, giving Rosalie enough recovery time to be more on guard when her introduction came.

'And this is Rebel's sister, Rosalie James.'

Politeness demanded she touch his hand. He seized complete possession of hers, strong fingers wrapping around it, pressing a hot imprint that felt like a claim on her entire body—his for the taking.

Resistance burned in her mind.

Nobody took her. Nobody!

'Her sister?' The assault of his eyes was briefly halted by a flicker of surprise at the relationship. He glanced at Rebel, then back to Rosalie, frowning.

'No likeness,' she dryly interpreted.

Celeste piped up. 'Everyone in Rebel's family was adopted, Mr. Cazell. From all over the world. Rebel is the English one...'

'And you?' he asked Rosalie, his eyes as sharp as steel knives.

Every instinct screamed to deny him any private information. She sensed he would maul it unmercifully. 'My life is my own, Mr. Cazell,' she said with quiet dignity.

'Adam,' he insisted.

She denied him the familiarity. Give this man an inch and he'd take a mile, and Rosalie was not about to travel his road which she'd already judged to be totally centred on what he wanted. She tore her gaze from his to send a quelling message to her chatterbox niece.

'Let's give Cate the chance to talk to her father,

Celeste. She hasn't seen him for…how long has it been, Cate?'

It was a deliberate barb, aimed at hitting some paternal guilt. Frustratingly, his daughter defused it. 'Oh, Dad will get around to me in his own good time,' she answered off-handedly.

Surprisingly Adam Cazell laughed, released Rosalie's hand and swung towards his daughter, spreading his arms invitingly. 'I could do with a hug, Catie mine.'

Her young face lit up with joy in the openly affectionate invitation. She flew at him and he lifted her up and whirled her around. 'Dad, I'm not a little kid anymore,' she protested, mindful of her dignity in this company but loving his uninhibited pleasure in her nonetheless.

He set her down with a look of helpless dismay. 'The terrible teens,' he moaned. 'You're only one small step into it. Does everything have to change?'

She huffed an exasperated sigh at him. 'You have to face the fact I'm growing up.'

'Well, you can teach me about it over the holidays,' he said with grand generosity.

'Sure.' Her mouth twisted. 'A few weeks to pack it all in.'

The irony floated right past him. Or he chose to ignore it, smiling to dispel the slightly sour note. 'So what have you two been doing this past week?' A twinkling look at Celeste. 'Shall we sit down and you can regale me with teenage girl things?'

Quite a charmer, Rosalie thought, watching Celeste's eager response to the invitation. They all moved to the lounge setting near the windows. With the confidence of a charismatic king, Adam Cazell proceeded to court his daughter and the family whose guest she still was until after lunch.

Rosalie had chosen an armchair slightly apart from the rest of them, determined on observing rather than participating. She knew he was aware of her detachment and would undoubtedly try to breach it sooner or later, which would put her on her mettle again, but she felt safe enough to watch him for a while, and he was quite compellingly watchable.

The charm tempered an innate forcefulness that obviously fuelled everything he tackled, explaining why he succeeded in whatever he undertook in the business world. And he was attractive, as well. Not in any pretty playboy sense. His face was too rugged to be called classically handsome but its strong lines and angles had a very male appeal that Rosalie judged would automatically evoke a positive response in both men and women. Besides which, the rather unruly waves of his dark hair softened the craggy look, adding to his charm, making him appear approachable.

The boys certainly weren't frightened of him.

More fascinated.

As they'd been by Zachary Lee.

The comparison niggled at Rosalie's sense of rightness. Adam Cazell might have the same formidable height and breadth of chest and shoulder as her big brother, promising a strength that would be easy to lean on, but she was sure he was much more a taker by nature than a giver.

She rubbed at the hand he had taken, wanting to erase the lingering sense of his invasive power. He noticed the action and she instantly stopped it, not wanting him to have the satisfaction of knowing he'd left his *touch* on her.

She wasn't sure if it was sex or ego driving him where she was concerned—maybe both. She'd been targeted by too many wealthy and influential men not to recognise that Adam Cazell fancied acquiring her, which, of course, was for the purpose of public show and sex on call until the gloss wore off and desire waned.

Usually such attention was water off a duck's back to Rosalie. But there was something more intense, more personal, more threatening about Adam Cazell. As much as she wanted to dismiss him, it was like he'd burrowed under her skin and she couldn't pry him out. Maybe if she watched him long enough, the disturbing effect of the man would fade.

Oddly enough, his daughter had made a strong impression on her, too. Cate was very bright, older than her years in reading people and where she stood with them. The occasional flash of cynicism in some of her comments had disturbed Rosalie, revealing knowledge bred by disappointment or disillusionment. Cate had grown armour she shouldn't need to have at thirteen.

But a privileged background didn't guarantee a happy upbringing. Celeste, who still looked angelic with her beautiful fair hair and big blue eyes, had been characterised by Hugh as 'an evil seed,' a monstrous child—expelled from one school after another for outrageous behaviour—before Rebel came into their lives and turned everything around for them. Rebel had seen Hugh's orphaned niece as a lost child in desperate need of rescue and had barged straight into proving to Hugh how wrong he was in his reading of the situation.

Rosalie didn't see Cate Cazell as being in need of rescue. She was a survivor, that one, probably with as strong a will as her father. She'd inherited his dark wavy hair, and the shape of his face—the high wide brow and the sharply delineated chisel chin, but her mouth was softer and her eyes were a warmer grey with a ring of amber around the irises. She was tall, too, though with a much more slender frame than her father. Rosalie imagined she'd be very striking when she grew up.

But for now, the girl did crave more of her father's time and attention. And should have it, Rosalie thought, remembering how much it had meant to her to have Zachary Lee caring about her every thought and feeling, loving her, protecting her, making her feel safe and secure. Not alone.

Yes…that was how Cate felt…too much alone. Her family consisted of a socialising mother, too busy aiding and abetting her political husband's career to actually listen to her daughter, a stepfather who was never *there* for her, a father who flew into and out of her life, handing out oodles of ice-cream, but not staying around long enough to realise that sweets weren't enough. No wonder Cate liked being with Celeste's family!

'Rosalie...'

His voice sliding into her private reverie, kicking her heart into a faster beat...the silver bullet eyes trained on her again, commanding her attention.

'I just remembered where I last saw you,' he said with a musing little smile designed to tease her interest.

Modelling put her in the public eye. It was not remarkable that she had been seen somewhere by Adam Cazell, possibly accompanying one of his girlfriends to a fashion show. Was this another attempt to dig into her life?

'The premiere of Turandot at the Met in New York,' he went on, surprising her with the venue named.

'You were there?' Rebel leapt in delightedly. 'You heard Zuang Chi sing?'

He nodded. 'A magnificent voice.'

'He's our brother,' Rebel claimed with pride. 'We were all there for his premiere. The whole family. It was a marvellous night, wasn't it, Rosalie?'

'Yes.'

She hadn't seen Adam Cazell at the opera and didn't like the feeling he had watched her without her knowing. Though she had been more or less on public exhibit that night, paid to wear the dress and necklace for others to see and covet.

He leaned forward on his sofa like a big cat about to pounce. 'Just how many are in your family, Rebel?'

She laughed. 'Fourteen of us. Plus husbands and wives and our wonderful parents. We filled a whole box at the Met, didn't we, darling?' She smiled at Hugh in fond recollection.

'We certainly did. Marvellous night,' he echoed.

Adam nodded in agreement. 'I'm sorry I didn't make your acquaintance at the time. Must confess I only noticed Rosalie.' His gaze sliced back to her, a wry little smile on his lips. 'You were singularly spectacular.'

She returned his smile. 'I was on parade.'

'And the red-haired man you were with?'

'Zachary Lee,' Rebel happily supplied. 'Our *big* brother.'

Satisfaction glinted in his eyes.

A possible competitor dismissed, Rosalie interpreted, thinking he had certainly noticed her escort, probably sizing him up and wondering how *attached* they were.

'None of us are blood relations,' she stated, feeling a strong urge to put a spoke in his wheel. 'That's why we don't look alike.'

'Uncle Zachary is the American one,' Celeste informed him.

'And the one we all look up to,' Rosalie quickly slid in, not wanting Celeste to list off their multinational family, which she was clearly on the verge of doing. A change of subject was urgently needed. 'Do you often attend the opera, Adam?' she inquired.

'No.'

'It was a premiere,' his daughter commented before he could add more. 'Daddy's girlfriends lu-u-uv premieres.'

'Oh, come on, Catie,' he chided good-naturedly. 'I've taken you to a few, too. The Harry Potter film, the…'

'Okay, okay.' She held up her hands in mock defence. 'He's far more into pop music, Rosalie. You know…Saturn Records before he sold it off? He didn't do classical stuff.'

'Which doesn't mean I can't enjoy it.' Slightly more snappish on that reply.

'I've never heard you play it,' Cate argued.

'You're not with me all the time.'

Big blunder.

Cate's face tightened. 'You're right, Dad. What do I get? Fifteen percent if I'm lucky? For all I know you could be playing opera all the time you don't have me with you.' She flashed a gritty look of apology at Rosalie. 'Sorry. Shouldn't have butted in. I can't *swear* my father doesn't like classical music.'

'Never a good idea to speak for others,' Rosalie tossed back with a sympathetic shrug.

Adam Cazell erased the frown evoked by Cate's

rather biting mockery, his sharply penetrating gaze targeting Rosalie again. 'Actually, a good voice attracts my attention regardless of what is being sung.'

'Then you must have enjoyed listening to Zuang Chi,' she replied, wondering if and how he would respond to his daughter's cry for more attention from him.

'To you, as well.'

'Me?' What did he mean? Had she lost the thread of this conversation while thinking about Cate.

His eyes burned into hers. 'I heard you sing at the Raffles Hotel Le Royal in Phnom Penh. You were leading a choir of orphans.'

Shock jammed her mind for several seconds. She struggled to take in the incredible coincidence of his actually being in the same place when... 'That was...nine months ago.'

'Yes,' he said. 'You have a beautiful singing voice. Very pure in tone.' His mouth quirked. 'If I'd still been running Saturn Records, I might have tried to sign you up.'

'Rosalie's birth mother was a professional singer,' Rebel remarked.

'I'm not interested,' she quickly cut in, shaking her head at her sister. 'You know that.'

Rebel sighed. 'It always seemed like a waste to me. Even Zuang Chi said...'

'No! I don't want to be in that world!' The curt dismissal effectively silenced her sister. She turned back to Adam Cazell who was learning—already knew—too much about her for Rosalie's comfort, digging, digging, digging. She turned the screw. 'What were you doing in Phnom Penh, Adam?'

'Scouting for my airline.'

His eyes mocked her evasive tactics.

Every muscle in her body tensed as she felt his intent to close in on her. Hunter...warrior...he embodied both those images in her mind, and for the first time in many many years, Rosalie felt vulnerable to a man.

Hugh's old butler made a timely entrance, announcing, 'Lunch is about to be served in the dining room, m'lord.'

'Thank you, Brooks.' Hugh stood up. 'Girls, boys, Adam...'

He ushered them out, leaving the two sisters to trail after them, a move that had undoubtedly been orchestrated by some telling look from his wife. Rosalie sometimes wondered if the understanding between them was almost psychic. At least, she was momentarily relieved of Adam Cazell's presence, but Rebel, of course, had something to say, linking arms with her for a confidential little chat.

'He's seriously aware of you, Rosalie. Totally captivated, I'd say,' she murmured.

'Rebel, I don't care to be the ornament on any man's arm.'

'I'm not suggesting you should be. I just think it's more than that. He's really interested.'

'He's a playboy. You've heard Cate rattle off all his girlfriends.'

'Well, maybe you should take off some time to play, too.'

Rosalie frowned at her sister. 'Why are you selling him to me?' Rebel had been a super saleswoman before she'd married Hugh and started a family.

A sigh. 'I'm worried about Cate. You must have caught those touches of bitterness when she was speaking to her father. Maybe you could do some good there, Rosalie.'

'Cate Cazell is not a lost child, Rebel. She's strong enough to fight her own battles with her father. I thought she got in a couple of good jabs today.'

'A parent can brush these things off, telling themselves the child is being moody, difficult. None so blind as those who don't want to see, Rosalie. But you could make him see through your eyes. And he'd listen to you. It's not right that Cate feels... abandoned.'

'I don't want to get involved with him.'

'It needn't be a heavy involvement.'

'He'll come onto me hard and fast. I know he will, given half a chance.'

'But you're so practised at holding men off.'

'He's different.'

'Oh?' Rebel looked fascinated.

Rosalie grimaced. 'Don't look at me like that. I know when something's not safe. I *know*.'

A frown. 'I thought you could handle anything.

Sorry for pressing. It's just…I am worried about Cate.
She's entering her teens. If she doesn't get what she
needs from her father…'

'She does have a mother.'

'Useless. Too full of her own life. It's Adam she
looks to. If he's not there for her…'

'Cate will manage in her own way.'

'No. She'll be at risk. If she feels let down and
alone…getting into drugs is a very easy step.'

'Why don't you speak to Adam yourself about
this?'

'I'm not the one he wants to win.'

Their private chat ended on that line. They'd entered the dining room and the others were there waiting for them to come and sit down.

Adam Cazell's gaze raked Rosalie from head to
foot, making her extremely conscious of the strip of
bare skin between her hipster jeans and the waist-
length blue and white striped bandeau top she wore,
her long hair loose over bare shoulders, her face bare
of make-up. She felt her blood heating, her pale skin
flushing.

She wanted to scream, 'No! Look elsewhere, Adam
Cazell.'

But he wasn't going to.

Cate stood beside him, not impinging on his consciousness one bit. It didn't occur to him that winning
his daughter was more important than winning another woman.

Rebel was right.

She did have the power to make him listen to her if he had the ears to hear.

Maybe she could handle the risk…for Catie's sake.

It shouldn't take long to hammer the message home.

CHAPTER THREE

SUNDAY lunch at Davenport Hall was always held in the informal dining room and very much a family affair. Regardless of any guests and despite their young age, the boys sat up at the table with their parents, Geoffrey with an extra cushion on his chair, Malcolm with a booster seat on his. They were only five and three but had been thoroughly coached in good manners, and Celeste at thirteen, was very much the young lady.

It was a lovely, bright, inviting room. The furniture was white, the furnishings yellow, and long windows overlooked a rose garden in full summer bloom. The pristine white cloth on the oval table showed off the centrepiece bowl of yellow rosebuds, and yellow linen serviettes in silver holders added their splash of colour. Rosalie sat between the boys, directly across from Adam Cazell who was flanked by the girls, Rebel and Hugh at the two ends.

Adam looked totally bemused as he watched the boys remove their serviettes from the holders and spread them on their laps. No doubt, in the company he usually kept, little children were segregated from the adults, not part of his world at all. Welcome to a

34

real family, Rosalie thought, and wondered if he'd learn anything from it.

The girls dominated the conversation, telling Adam about their last school term—teachers they liked or disliked, hockey matches, tattle about other girls in their class. He indulged their eager chatter, smiling, laughing, frowning quizzically in all the right places. It seemed effortless on his part—no act—no hint of condescension.

He was charming.

And very, very attractive.

Possibly putting himself out to be so because she was observing him.

He shared flashes of amusement with her but made no concerted attempt to engage her in personal conversation. Biding his time, she thought, probably hoping the happy casual atmosphere at the table would lower her guard enough to let him slide inside it later. Having been on the international model circuit since she was eighteen—eleven years now—Rosalie was too experienced with men of his ilk not to know how they made their moves.

When the first strike didn't produce a warm response, set up more favourable circumstances and try a more subtle approach. Few gave up at the first knock-back. Most of them simply didn't believe it. Why would any woman reject such a prize? Only to increase her value and force a chase. But the chase didn't last long. If the desired result wasn't fast in coming, there was always another beautiful woman for such men. Much better for the ego to be appreciated than feel defeated.

Adam Cazell's next move came after lunch. Coffee had been served in the sitting room. The girls had gone upstairs to complete Cate's packing for her departure. Rebel had taken Malcolm up to the nursery for an afternoon nap. Geoffrey was occupying Hugh's attention.

Adam rose from his chair, saying, 'Would you mind if I went for a stroll in your grounds, Hugh? Stretch my legs before driving back to London.'

'Not at all.' Being the thoughtful host he was, his head instantly swung to Rosalie. 'Will you show Adam around?' A rueful smile. 'I doubt Geoffrey has the legs for two long walks.'

Trapped by courtesy.

A clever manouvre from Adam Cazell.

But she was safe in the grounds of Davenport Hall, Rosalie swiftly reasoned, pushing up from her chair to oblige her brother-in-law's guest. And suddenly the silver-bullet eyes were dancing wickedly at her, jolting her confidence and quickening her pulse.

'Is there a maze we can get lost in?' he tossed at her.

'No. But there's a lake you could drown in,' she flipped back at him.

He laughed, his face crinkling, turning up the wattage of his attraction. Rosalie felt her hands clenching in an instinctive need to fight the power that flowed so strongly from him. She had to make a conscious effort to relax her muscles, pretend she was unaffected.

'We'll go out the back way,' she said, and led out into the hallway where he quickly stepped up beside her.

'Are there canoes?' he asked.

She arched an eyebrow at him. 'Didn't you say you wanted to stretch your legs?'

He grinned. 'Canoeing is very physical. You could sit at the other end while I do all the work.'

'The canoes are all one-seaters.'

'You're dashing my romantic dream. Here I am in an old-world setting, in the company of a beautiful woman…'

'And you have a daughter who doesn't want you to be distracted from her,' Rosalie reminded him.

'Ah! The carer of children's needs. I guess this comes from having been orphaned yourself.'

He could turn on a pin. Of course, he had to have an agile and astute mind to be so successful at what he did, and his focus was all on her at the moment, driving to win. Somehow she had to force a refocussing if she was to achieve anything for Cate.

'A child needs to feel someone cares enough to be there for them. Do you think your daughter feels that, Adam?'

'At last she uses my name,' he lightly mocked. 'But does this mean she's warming to me? No. She's using it to emphasise the point that's important to her.'

His accurate analysis made her respect his brain even more. She slanted him a challenging look. 'You haven't answered me.'

'Nor have you, me, Rosalie James,' he swiftly countered, his eyes stabbing her with that truth.

Tit for tat.

Having walked through the hall, they stepped out into the afternoon sunshine and started down the path that led to the ornamental lake. The lawns on either side of it were a lush green. Banks of rhododendrons lent spectacular colour. Waterlilies added their exotic charm. It was a very English scene, Rosalie thought, and knew Rebel had found her home here with Hugh.

She felt completely rootless, herself. No city or country had any special call on her heart. People, yes, but not a place. She wondered if the jet-setting Adam Cazell considered one place home. According to Cate he had residences in London, New York, Hong Kong, and on a Caribbean island. The latter was probably for some taxation alleviation.

'Do you live here with your sister?' he asked.

'No. Just visiting this past week.'

'Where do you call home?'

Rosalie shrugged. 'Nowhere in particular. There are places I can stay whenever I want to.'

'You must have a base from which you work.'

Trying to pin her down. Wanting to know where he could find her. Rosalie wasn't about to make it easy for him though he was right. She had a base in London, the Mayfair apartment owned by Joel Faber, her sister Tiffany's husband. Joel had insisted any one of the James family could use it whenever they wanted to. He'd appointed her the apartment-sitter, knowing full well where most of her money went and wanting to help her in her mission.

'I don't have many possessions,' she said. 'I have no need of them.'

'Are you telling me they can be kept in a suitcase?' he asked sceptically.

'Just about.' She threw him a taunting look. 'I probably fly around the world as much as you do, Adam Cazell.'

'Which gives us something in common.'

'The difference is, I don't have a daughter who's left alone.'

'Cate is not alone. She has her school, as Celeste does. Her mother and stepfather never leave England. She can be with them, call on them…'

'They have other priorities,' Rosalie cut in, shooting him a look that told him he should know that. 'Just because they're here does not mean they are readily available to her. Any more than you are.'

His mouth twisted sardonically. 'You're accusing me of neglect.'

'I'm telling you how it is for her.'

'You've known my daughter for what…all of one week? A bit presumptuous, don't you think, Rosalie?'

'I'm sure you'd like to believe that. Much easier to dismiss what I'm saying.'

His voice took on an edge of anger as he sought a

reason for her argument. 'She's been playing poor little rich girl to you?'

'No. Cate has too much pride for that.'

'Then why are you attacking me?' His eyes sliced at hers. 'Is this your best form of defence?'

'Defence against what?'

He halted. Since she was committed to being his companion on this walk, it forced her to pause and cast an inquiring glance at him. It was easier to ignore the power of the man while walking side by side but standing still, she immediately felt swamped by the intense energy force he emitted, and his strong air of command was reinforced by the blazing certainty in his eyes.

'That's not worthy of you, Rosalie James.'

Her heart missed a beat then leapt into a wild pounding. 'I beg your pardon?' she prevaricated.

'If you're trading truth, then don't lie about what you're feeling with me. It destroys your credibility.'

He was throwing down his gauntlet. Rosalie threw down hers. 'Okay. You'd like my suitcase in your hall for a while. I prefer to pass on that.'

'You can't put what I want in a suitcase. I don't care if you dress up or not.'

She raised her eyebrows mockingly. 'No ornamental display?'

'Irrelevant.'

'Just the *naked* truth.'

His eyes derided her reading of him. 'That I would like, but not in the limited sense you mean.'

A convulsive little shiver ran down her spine as she felt his purpose to invade far more than her body. Rosalie fiercely argued to herself that she was a curiosity to him, an enigma in his kind of world, and he'd teased himself into wanting to know what made her tick. She didn't stop to examine what she felt towards him because it was too threatening to her peace of mind.

'I don't have time for you, Adam.'

'Make time.'

The sheer magnetism of the man tugged at her. She'd felt nothing like this before with anyone. It was as though he was claiming her, and all her self-protective instincts rose to fight any surrender to his will.

'*You* make time…for your daughter,' she hurled back at him.

It did not hit any discernible mark. 'I do,' he replied, still maintaining an implacable concentration on her. 'I take Cate with me during her school holidays. During term I send her postcards from wherever I am. She can call me on my mobile telephone whenever she likes.'

'She's been *here* for the first week of her summer holidays.'

'Not because I failed to be available. It was her choice.'

'And what does that choice say to you, Adam? What does your daughter get with Celeste's family that she doesn't get with you?'

'Since you're bursting to tell me...tell me.'

Rosalie paused, the challenge ringing in her ears, demanding truths that he could recognise, take on board. He was not as much at fault as she had assumed where Cate was concerned. Her mind flitted through all the silent criticisms she had made, trying to home in on the basic problem.

'She's flaunting it in your face, Adam.'

'What?'

'Secure ground that's not going to change.'

He frowned, grimaced, made a gesture encompassing the grounds around them. 'This is not my life. Any more than it's yours. I can't change who I am.'

'She craves what Celeste has—a place to come home to, being an integral part of a family where children are a blessing not a nuisance to be accommodated.'

'I have never treated Cate as a nuisance.' Vehement denial.

'What of your girlfriends? Cate mentioned a string of them. When you have your daughter with you, do you spend much time with her one on one, or is she an extra?'

Another frown. 'She's never seemed to mind when I've had a companion.'

'What choice does she have but to fit in...if she wants to be with you?'

'I take her wherever she wants to go. We have a lot of fun together.'

'You entertain her.'

'Something wrong with that?' he rumbled as though barely holding back an explosion of frustration with her argument.

'It's froth and bubble, Adam. It doesn't ease the loneliness inside. The sense of being a floating part of your life, not of any prime consideration, is eating away at Cate. If you really care about her, take her somewhere special these holidays—just the two of you—and get to know her as a person. She's thirteen. She needs to feel someone loves her for who she is inside.'

He reined in the anger that had been simmering. His eyes scoured hers, searching for ulterior motives to attach to her diatribe against him. There were none. Rosalie stood her ground, waiting for his response, willing him to give her what she needed.

'Why do you care so much?' he asked gruffly.

'Who will if I don't?'

He shook his head. 'Catie is not your business.'

'Caring for children is my business, Adam.'

'She's not an orphan.'

'She's in need.'

He frowned, but he didn't refute what she'd said, which might or might not be a step forward. His expression hardened and his narrowed eyes flashed a cynical look at her. 'Who knows the person you are inside, Rosalie?'

'My family.'

'All fourteen of your brothers and sisters and the people who adopted you?'

'Some more, some less. Overall we're a very close-knit unit, supportive of each other.'

She was arguing Cate's cause because Rebel had asked it of her, though she was sympathetic to it, as well. Oddly enough, she no longer felt so antagonistic towards Adam Cazell. He was not a bad father. Given the man he was and the life he led, he'd certainly made the effort to be a presence in his daughter's life.

His mouth tilted into a wry little smile as he commented, 'Then you're very fortunate…in your family.'

He turned his head, gazing out over the lake, and she sensed his withdrawal from her. He stood a man apart, strongly self-contained, yet possibly he felt very alone on his pinnacle of singular achievement. She wondered about him, whether he'd had parents who'd made the time to know him, siblings who were brought up with him, sharing. What of his ex-wife, his girlfriends…had they ever touched his heart…his soul?

Observing him wrapped in his own thoughts, she was struck by the idea he'd always walked alone, knew nothing else. A man like him had few peers, and those that were would be in contest with him. That was the nature of the beast. As for the women in his life, had any of them seen past what he could give them? Huge wealth and the power that went with it might have been enough for them.

Perhaps she'd been blinded by it herself in making her judgment of him. Impulsively she stepped closer and touched his arm to bring him back from wherever he'd gone. 'You and Cate could form a wonderful bond if you reached out to her,' she pressed.

His biceps muscle tensed. His gaze fastened on hers, bypassing her plea with a piercing intensity that demanded something far more personal. 'What of us?' he shot out, his other hand lifting to grasp her arm.

It was like an electric jolt zapping through her.

Shocked, immobilised, mind jammed, Rosalie could only stare back at him.

'Why trust Cate with me when *you* haven't taken the time to know *the person I am inside,* Rosalie James?'

The words punched into her heart.

The need pulsing from him took her breath away.

Then something deep and alien to her stirred inside Rosalie, a sexual awakening that she had never expected to experience, a wanting to know this man in every sense, a yearning for the kind of love she knew existed between her sisters and the men they'd married. Yet even as she felt this, panic screamed into her mind, beating up the fearful thought—*it's not safe!*

'Da...ad!' came the exasperated call from his daughter.

His jaw tightened. His eyes bit into hers with ruthless and relentless purpose. 'Don't think I'll walk out of your life, Rosalie. We'll meet again.'

She was left shaken to the core as he released her

arm. Her own hand slid limply from his as he turned to face Cate who'd started down the path towards them and now stood waiting, her arms folded with an air of impatience. Or was it resentment that he'd gone off with yet another woman instead of waiting for her?

She'd seen them touching.

Rosalie struggled to block what Adam had said to her out of her mind...focus on the child who was no longer really a child. Her legs carried her automatically, keeping pace with Adam's. They walked apart, but the sense of an inevitable link with him could not be broken.

They reached Cate.

Adam put an arm around his daughter's shoulders and the stiffness instantly went out of them. He hugged her close, smiling, chatting, and she glowed up at him, loving his attention.

He didn't speak to Rosalie again, not in any personal sense. He said a general goodbye to the family, thanking them for their hospitality. All of them trooped out to watch him and Cate drive away from Davenport Hall, the car moving slowly down the avenue of giant elms, as though being gradually drawn through a tunnel to a different time and place.

Rosalie felt a strange tug on her heart.

Into her mind flashed the thought... *I should be with them.*

But it wasn't her journey, she swiftly told herself.

Then Rebel hooked onto her arm and asked, 'Did you do any good?'

She managed an offhand smile. 'I tried.'

'Then he'll make it work,' her sister said with confidence.

Rosalie didn't comment. Rebel had a way of reading things right and Adam Cazell *was* the kind of man who made things work when he set his mind to it.

We'll meet again.

Was that good or bad?

Impossible to know at this point.

Her only certainty was that somewhere in her future, Adam Cazell would walk back into her life and she would have to deal with it, one way or another.

CHAPTER FOUR

ADAM'S mind was greatly exercised by the enigma of Rosalie James as he drove away from Davenport Hall. He felt pumped up by the certainty that she was attracted to him, even against her will, and that will was very, very strong. But why was she so guarded against him? What was she hiding? And how was he going to pry her secrets into the open where he could deal with them?

Beside him, Cate heaved a deeply felt sigh.

Guilt stabbed into Adam. He should be thinking of her, making appropriate plans to deal with the problem he hadn't known about until Rosalie James had laid it on him.

'Sorry to be leaving or glad to be off and away with me?' he tossed at her lightly.

The only response was a private grimace, no return glance at him. 'I guess I can't blame you,' came the resigned mutter. 'She's very beautiful. Even I keep looking at her when she's anywhere in sight.'

'I take it you're speaking of Rosalie James.'

'Who else?' A dry little taunt. 'I'd have to say she's a class above all the other women you've had.'

'I agree she's different,' he said slowly, resisting

the strong temptation to pump his daughter for information on the woman who so intrigued him.

They'd both spent the past week at Davenport Hall, in a family environment where normal barriers would be down, and Celeste would undoubtedly have satisfied any curiosity Cate had wanted answered about the aunt who was a megastar in the fashion world. But newly alert to what Cate might be thinking and feeling, Adam forced himself to focus on the tone and import of what she was saying.

'Have you disliked the women I've had as companions?' he asked.

She shrugged. 'It's not a matter of whether I like or dislike them, is it? I mean...you never ask me. I just get landed with them.'

'Have you found that difficult?'

She brooded in silence for a while.

They left the village of Milton Prior behind. The Aston Marton ate up the road. Adam had plenty to think about as he drove on, waiting for a reply.

It had never occurred to him to ask his daughter's permission to bring any woman of his choice into their lives. He had needs, too, he argued to himself, and Cate had to accept that. He certainly wasn't about to be celibate for the rest of his life. But maybe he should become more aware of how she related to the company he kept. Perhaps he had been too blasé about doing what he wanted, not considering how much he expected Cate to simply fit in.

'I wouldn't mind Rosalie,' she finally said, somewhat grudgingly.

'So you have minded having the others around,' he concluded.

She rolled her eyes at him. 'They're only there for you. You're not that dumb, Dad. They put up with me to have you.'

'Have any of them been nasty to you?'

'Of course not. They're not dumb, either. Usually they do all sorts of stuff to keep me sweet. After all, I am your daughter.'

The cynical flavour of her words struck a bad chord with Adam. Cate was only just thirteen and already she was standing back and assessing people through jaundiced eyes. It shouldn't be like this. But how could he protect her from it? He was who he was and that wasn't going to change.

'Why wouldn't you mind Rosalie James?'

Again she pondered before answering. 'It's a funny thing about Rosalie,' she said as though musing out loud. 'You'd think she'd be full of herself. You know...with how she looks and who she is. The girls at school would just die if she ever visited. I mean she's really huge on the modelling scene and just so stunningly beautiful for real. It's not make-up or clever photography.'

'So I noticed,' he acknowledged dryly.

'But it's like...' Cate looked earnestly at him, wanting him to understand the picture she was drawing. '...none of that is important to her. She shrugs it off as though it's just something she does because she was lucky enough to be born with those looks. No big deal. And you can tell she gets quickly bored if you ask her about it, because before you know it, she turns the conversation around, and you find you're talking about yourself.'

'Well, that's a good trick to protect your privacy.'

'Mmmh...' She frowned, then shook her head. 'I don't think it's a trick.'

'Why not?'

'Because she really listens. It's like...she sees where you're coming from and understands. If it was a trick, what you told her wouldn't mean anything. It would just float by her. Like it does with Mum.' Her voice took on a disturbing edge of contempt. 'Who pretends to listen but you know her mind is off somewhere else.'

He frowned. 'You've got a communication problem with your mother?'

'Duh...' she drawled, her tone of disrespect seeming to encompass him, as well.

Adam didn't like it. He had to remind himself that respect was earned, not a given, even with one's parents. Hadn't he retreated from his own in his teens, realising the generation gap had become impossible to cross? They hadn't had a clue what he was about. They'd marched to a different drum. The easiest course had been to play to their image of how their son should act, and pursue his own path behind their backs.

It was a sobering thought when linked to his daughter.

Cate gave a derisive little laugh. 'Talking to Mum is like talking to that cockatoo in the TV ad.'

'What TV ad?'

A sigh. 'Of course. You don't have time to watch TV.'

'So tell me about it,' Adam invited, ignoring the point of difference in their lifestyles.

'This woman gets a phone call from a friend who's obviously dumping stuff on her and she doesn't want to listen. So she puts the receiver next to her pet cockatoo who's sitting on a perch, and every so often the cockatoo crows into the receiver, "I know. I know." Then finally, "I know, dear." It's a hoot.'

The mimic of the bird's voice was too much like Sarah's for Adam's comfort. He'd have to speak to his ex-wife about this, warn her she was losing Cate through lack of attention.

'The ad is for chocolate, which the woman proceeds to eat,' she went on. 'Pretty clever, huh? Much more enjoyable to consume than a load of stuff that has nothing to do with your life.'

'Very clever.'

Point taken. And very aptly put, Adam thought, aware that Sarah was very wrapped up in pushing her husband's political career, doing everything possible on the social side to promote it. Cate was an appendage, not a prime focus. Just as she was to him, Adam conceded, but an appendage he did give consideration to. It was the quality of the consideration that was in question here.

He wondered how much of this Rosalie James had listened to. And *heard*. His respect for her went up several notches. It would have taken courage, too, to tackle him as she had with a barrage of unpalatable truths.

Cate gave him a look that carried a shrewd calculation that instantly put Adam on his mettle. 'Did you do a line on her?' she asked.

'Who?'

'Rosalie James.'

He found himself inwardly recoiling from the cynical flavour of the question. There was nothing cynical about the feelings stirred by *this* woman and he didn't want to answer Cate in such crass terms.

'Or do you have someone waiting back in London?' she pushed when he didn't immediately answer, her tone flattening out with disinterest in anyone else.

'No. I'm not involved with anyone at the moment.'

In fact, no one since Sacha, whose attraction had died a quick death after the night at the opera. Same with Tahlia after the night in Phnom Penh. Not that any particular fault lay with either woman. In both instances it had been difficult to get Rosalie James out of his mind.

'Well?' Cate persisted. 'You got her out in the grounds alone.'

No doubt about his capacity to arrange whatever

he wanted. How many times had Cate observed him...*doing a line?* Did she feel like a spectator in his life, not a participant?

'Rosalie wanted to speak to me privately. About you,' he stated, knowing that was the only reason for her accompanying him. Her resistance to what he wanted had been rock-solid. Though possibly he had made some dent in it.

'Me?' Cate was astounded.

'Mmmh...' He threw her a smile. 'She likes you. Very much.'

Her face bloomed with colour. Adam wasn't sure if it was pleasure or embarrassment. She quickly turned her head and gazed out the side window. Her hands fidgeted in her lap.

'What did she say?'

He chose his words with care, wanting to establish a new basis for understanding between them. 'That you're extremely smart and I should learn more about you instead of taking you for granted.' He paused to let this concept sink in before adding, 'It struck me as a good idea. So I thought we might spend these summer holidays on Tortola, just relaxing together and doing whatever we fancy. How does that strike you?'

Her head whipped around, her eyes very bright. 'You mean...just the two of us?'

He smiled. 'Yes. Just the two of us.'

'No friends or executives dropping in?' Disbelief in her voice.

'None. I will have to spend an hour or two each day in the computer room, but apart from that, I'm all yours, Catie. We can go shopping in London tomorrow, buy whatever clothes you need, arm ourselves with some new games to play, books to read, then off to the Caribbean. What say you?'

'Yessss!' she almost yelled with excitement, her hands clapping in pure joy. 'That will be terrific, Dad!'

He laughed, happy to have made her happy. 'We'll have a good time.'

'We sure will.'

'But we definitely need some new games. You always beat me at Scrabble.'

'That's because you don't take long enough to think what might score more than the first word you see in your letters.'

'Uh-huh! Then be warned. I shall *think* in future.'

Cate laughed and bubbled with plans.

Rosalie James was forgotten.

But not by Adam.

There wasn't going to be another woman in his life.

Until *she* accepted that position.

CHAPTER FIVE

ROSALIE was organising her packing for the next trip when the telephone rang. She picked up the receiver without any thought of who might be calling, her mind still occupied with the job ahead of her—what was required for it, how much time it would take.

'Rosalie James,' she rattled out automatically.

'Adam Cazell.'

The deep timbre of his voice rolled through her heart like a drum, heralding something momentous. Shock held her rigid and speechless. It was almost a month since their meeting at Davenport Hall. She'd been to Thailand and back, mostly succeeding in shutting him and his daughter out of her mind.

But the shockwave still hitting her now wasn't from just hearing his voice. It was feeling his presence at the other end of the line, reaching out and seizing her whole consciousness, obliterating everything else. The sense of being under siege was instant and overwhelming.

'I want to thank you for the very good advice you gave me the last time we met,' he said warmly, triggering a flood of heat that unsettled her further.

She took a deep breath and fought for calm composure. 'How did you get this number, Adam?' she asked, doing her best to project coolness.

'From your sister,' he answered easily.

'Rebel gave it to you?'

'Any reason why she shouldn't?'

Celeste and Cate...best friends...the personal connection. Rebel probably hadn't thought the rule of privacy applied in this case.

'I did mention how much I appreciated your help with Cate,' he went on. 'And that is absolutely genuine, Rosalie.'

It pricked her interest. 'You've built up a closer rapport with her?'

'It's been a rewarding few weeks.'

'I'm glad to hear it.'

'I thought you might like to come and see for yourself.'

Another meeting. Of course this was his motive for calling. Cate was a complete side issue. He was attacking on a subtle front, planning to segue into her life again through his daughter, and despite knowing this, perhaps because of it, the tug to meet them both again was strong.

Except it wouldn't stop there.

Adam Cazell would mount a campaign to draw her into his life, and she might very well lose herself to this man. And where would she be then? She didn't want to be *owned* by anyone. Personal control was important to her. The freedom to do what she wanted when she could plan it was important to her.

'Cate and I are on Tortola, Rosalie,' he informed, breaking into her fevered thoughts. 'It's one of the British Virgin Islands in the Caribbean. I have a villa here.'

Far away, she thought in relief. He wasn't about to knock on her door, compelling a decision that threw her into conflict with all she'd been up until now.

'Cate and I have spent the past few weeks just lazing around together. We've talked a lot. We'd both like you to come and visit us. Stay a week. Relax and enjoy yourself.'

It was a very seductive invitation…a week on a Caribbean island. She'd never heard of Tortola. It couldn't be one of the more touristy islands. A private retreat, she thought. No paparazzi taking photographs, stirring gossip. She shouldn't feel so tempted. It wasn't possible anyway.

'Thank you, but I have a professional commitment, Adam. I'm flying to New York tomorrow morning to do a photo shoot.'

'How long will that take?'

'A few days,' she answered evasively, resisting the sense of being pinned down.

'It's not far from New York to Tortola. I can have my private plane standing by to fly you down. All you need do is call the Saturn Company office in New York, give your name, and arrangements will be made to transport you here as soon as your work is done.'

Her heart fluttered at the pressure being applied. The urge to go and have done with Adam Cazell in a limited time-frame and out of the public eye, warred with the fear of being trapped in a situation from which there'd be no easy escape.

'I promise you that coming here would not commit you to anything you don't want, Rosalie,' he said in a gentler tone, subtly persuasive. 'Cate can be a chaperone. Is that *safe* enough for you?'

Nothing felt safe with him. 'I barely know you, Adam,' she temporised.

'But you know Cate. Knew her better than I did,' he reminded her. 'And I'm not about to do anything to harm the understanding I've reached with my daughter.'

'Surely she'd prefer to have you to herself.'

'Cate is as much behind this invitation as I am,' came the swift reply.

'I don't think I believe that.'

'Come and find out for yourself.'

Again the strong tug.

'She likes you,' he went on, beating at her resolve to stay clear of the danger he posed. 'And I want to know you, Rosalie. I think you want to know me, too.'

Her stomach contracted. All the muscles around the centre of her sexuality tightened. She did want to know how it would be as a woman with *this* man. And she wanted to know why he affected her so...so uncontrollably. Perhaps, in knowing she could better deal with it.

'Why not give us this opportune time together?' he pressed.

Why not?

A few days of his company might settle this problem with him once and for all. Yet something very basic in her rebelled against surrendering to his will.

'I'll think about it,' she said. 'A short visit to Tortola may fit in. It may not.'

'I won't go away, Rosalie,' he said softly, insidiously.

It was more a statement of fact than a threat. Was he so sure of having invaded her life to such a deep extent she couldn't drive him out? How could he know that she felt him hovering in her consciousness, waiting for entry, pressing for entry?

'No. I don't expect you will, Adam Cazell,' she conceded. 'But letting you in takes some thinking about. Please don't use this telephone number again without my personal permission.'

A small silence, loaded with the tension of him trying to read her mind. Then, 'I'm sorry if you consider this call an unwelcome intrusion. It wasn't meant to be.'

'I prefer to decide whose calls are welcome and whose aren't. Don't use my sister, Adam. Or anyone else in my family.'

'Agreed.'

'Thank you for the invitation. I *will* think about it.'

She hung up, ending the call before he could say anything else, satisfied that she had won some control over the situation. She needed to feel that with him. Especially with him. Because he wasn't going to go away and she had to deal with the disturbance he caused.

Adam heard the click, closing off the verbal connection, leaving him pondering a level of resistance he was not familiar with. Though he had anticipated it with her, couching the invitation in terms that should have won the result he wanted. And maybe it still would. She hadn't said no. The choice had been left open.

As he slowly replaced the receiver, Adam felt his body clenching with a desire so fierce that if Rosalie James had been standing in front of him, he would have charged into carrying her off to the closest bed where she'd have to admit to feeling the same compulsion to explore everything between them. Whatever was getting in the way of their coming together had to be smashed.

Or changed, he corrected with more sober thought. He knew in his bones that force would not achieve anything with Rosalie James, except to drive her further away from him. She might have a large family to support her in times of emotional need, but for the most part she pursued her own course alone and Adam guessed she didn't want the ties of a relationship with a man. He wondered if she'd ever been with any man.

Teasing thought…to be the first.

Though knowing her was far more the goal he had in mind. He'd get there, he told himself. If not here on Tortola, somewhere else.

He strolled out to the wide verandah that overlooked the cove. The emerald water glistened in the afternoon sunshine…beautiful, serene…a world away from the hustle and bustle of New York, the pressures of work, the perfect place to unwind, relax. She couldn't help but let her guard down here, Adam thought, willing her to make that choice.

'So is she coming?' Cate asked, pausing in setting out the game they'd agreed on playing, looking at him with bright, interested eyes.

'I don't know,' he answered honestly. 'She has a photo shoot in New York. She might fly down after that. Depends on how she feels, I guess.'

Cate shook her head at him. 'You're losing your touch, Dad.'

He shook his head back at her. 'I didn't expect Rosalie James to come running.'

'Mmmh…that makes her different, too. I bet you haven't had a girlfriend yet who hasn't grabbed at the chance.'

True enough.

Adam settled himself at the table where the game board and train cards had been laid out. They both enjoyed Union Pacific. It required strategy as well as luck to win, and Cate was a ferocious competitor, looking for every chance to block his progress.

'Disappointing though,' she added on a sigh.

'I think Rosalie James has her own agenda, Cate. She has to decide if she wants to include us in it or not.'

She gave him a calculating look. 'You could help her with the save the children stuff. Give her free tickets on your airline.'

'I wouldn't even suggest it to her.' He was absolutely certain she would freeze him out in no time flat if he tried that tactic.

'Might be a winning move.'

'No. Some people can't be bought, Cate. Rosalie James is one of them.'

She nodded. 'I think you're right. I wouldn't like her if she could be. You know, Mum mixes with a lot of people who are angling for something. They're not *real* friends.'

'I'm sure your mother knows that, too. They're called useful contacts in the political world.'

'I don't like it, Dad. It's all so…' She screwed up her nose in distaste. '…false.'

'Nothing we can do about it, Catie. That's how it works.'

Sarah should be explaining this, he thought, mitigating the impact of Cate's view of her mother's life by spending quality time with her, listening, straightening things out. When they returned to London he'd have to set up a meeting with his ex-wife, make her understand what was going on.

'I guess so,' Cate conceded dispiritedly.

'Come on. Let's play.'

'Okay.' She shrugged off her discontent and gave him a brilliant smile. 'Maybe Rosalie will come. That would be good, wouldn't it?'

'Yes, it would be good but we can't count on it.' No use feeding hope that might build to more disappointment. 'It's her choice.'

And that was a truth he might have to grapple with himself if Rosalie James continued to evade him. But if it was the last thing he did, he'd find out why.

Rosalie forced herself to finish packing for the New York trip. But her mind kept drifting to Tortola. She hovered at her clothes cupboard. A swimming costume? Some light casual gear? Just in case she decided...

It was crazy letting Adam Cazell get to her like this. From everything Cate had said he was a dyed-in-the-wool playboy and she hated the idea of being so...so drawn to such a man. The next woman in a queue—that was all she'd be to him. More of a challenge than most, which undoubtedly stoked his desire. Why was she even thinking of allowing it to happen?

Because...part of her wanted the experience and once it was over and done with, maybe she'd be able to get on with her life and not have to think about him anymore. Everyone said passion didn't last. And it wasn't really giving in to him. It would be a case of mutual consent...if she went to Tortola.

But she didn't feel *safe* about it.

If only Rebel hadn't given Adam her telephone

number…and why had she? It was an understood thing between them that it not be given out without first checking that it was okay with her. Better still to get a return number that Rosalie could ring herself if she wanted to.

She snatched up the receiver from her bedside table and dialled Davenport Hall. As it happened, her sister answered the call and Rosalie flew into attack mode. 'Why did you give Adam Cazell this number, Rebel?'

'What's wrong?' Instant concern.

'You know how I feel about my privacy.'

'I thought you'd want to hear that your advice to Adam about Cate had borne fruit.'

'You could have told me so yourself.'

'Rosalie…it seemed only right that you hear it from him. He was very appreciative, grateful…'

'This has nothing to do with Cate. He wants *me*, Rebel. And you know it. You told me so.'

'Did he ask you to meet him?'

'Yes, he did.'

'If you said no, I'm sure Adam Cazell will respect that decision.'

'He'll keep asking. I know he will.'

'Why are you afraid of him, Rosalie? He's not going to stalk you. He might well keep asking but you can always say no.'

She dragged in a deep breath, quelling the panic that had crept into her voice. 'You shouldn't have given him this number.'

A deep sigh. 'No, I guess I shouldn't and I'm sorry

it's upset you. The truth is…I like him. And while he has certainly been a playboy, some men don't know what they're missing until they find it. I think you would be safe with him.'

That was a huge statement. It momentarily took Rosalie's breath away. Then she rushed back into speech. 'You don't know what you're saying. Adam Cazell and I…we're very different people.'

'I thought the same thing about Hugh when we first met.'

'Rebel, you know where I come from.'

'Yes, and I can't help thinking it's shaped your whole life. And that's not right, Rosalie. There's more to being a woman than working as you do. Not that I have any criticism of what you achieve. I think it's wonderful that you care for and help so many children. But it's too…selfless.'

'It's not. It's the most rewarding thing I can do.'

'Okay. I won't argue with you on that. It's your life, your decision. I'm sorry I did the wrong thing for you. My only excuse is…I hoped it might be right.'

'Okay. Just please don't do it again.'

'The fortress gates are shut,' came the dry rejoinder. 'But I still think it's a shame you're leaving Adam Cazell out in the cold. At least, think about giving him a chance. He might be good for you.'

More to being a woman…

Good for you…

Safe with him…

Rebel's words kept whirling through her mind long into the night.

She didn't know what was true.

CHAPTER SIX

ADAM could not remember ever being so gripped with nervous tension as he watched the small Saturn plane touch down on Beef Island and head down the runway towards him. He had not heard personally from Rosalie James, but she was on board. Confirmation that she was on her way to Tortola had come through this morning. How long she would stay was not given. Which undoubtedly meant it would depend on what happened with him. And Cate.

They stood together, ready to welcome her. Cate had been bubbling with plans all morning—where they should go, what they should show Rosalie while she was here, choosing the guest suite she would have at the villa, making sure it looked welcoming with bowls of flowers in the bedroom and bathroom.

It was very clear to Adam that his daughter had made up her mind that if he had to be attached to a girlfriend, Rosalie James was her choice and she intended to do everything possible to encourage the relationship. The question was…would a happy Cate have the same pull on Rosalie as one who needed attention? Probably not in any long-term sense. She was a woman with a mission.

This was time out for her. Adam couldn't fool him-

self otherwise. But obviously she had decided to give
something of herself to him or she wouldn't have
come. So at least this visit was a start. To her it might
also be an end. Adam was very aware that he couldn't
assume it would comprise anything more than a visit,
but he was determined on pushing it as far as he
could. In every sense.

'I wonder what she'll be wearing,' Cate said somewhat breathlessly as the plane came to a halt.

'Doesn't matter,' Adam muttered, his gaze fastened
on the door that would soon be opened.

'But she is a top model, Dad. And coming straight
from a photo shoot. I bet she's got a whole stack of
glamorous clothes with her.'

'People who travel a lot, travel lightly. My guess
is she'll only bring one suitcase.'

'Bet you're wrong.'

'We'll see.'

His heart kicked into a faster beat as the door
opened and the exit steps moved down. She emerged,
wearing a floppy white hat and dark glasses that suc-
cessfully hid any facial expression. But the rest of her
looked surprisingly young—vulnerable, Adam instantly thought—and very feminine, dressed in a
white off the shoulder peasant blouse with ruffles
down the bodice, a black and white polka dot skirt
with a frilled hem, and a wide red belt curving around
her hips, accentuating her small waist.

'Wow! That's very *in!*' Cate declared admiringly.

But not glamorous. No intent to knock his eyes out.

This was a softer, more accessible Rosalie James. He couldn't even call the dark glasses and hat some form of protective armour against him. The heat and glaring sunlight justified wearing both.

Adam's tension eased as anticipation soared. The spring of confidence was in his step as he strode forward to greet her, a broad smile beaming his pleasure in her arrival. Cate quickly matched pace with him, as eager as he was to get this situation working well.

Having disembarked from the plane, Rosalie stayed by the steps, waiting for the flight attendant to bring out her luggage. She carried a compact black handbag, only big enough to contain a wallet, passport, some make-up, possibly a small hairbrush. As she looked up at the guy now descending the steps Adam saw that her long black hair was loose but encircled at the back of her neck by a red scrunchie.

'You're right, Dad. Only one suitcase and it's not big,' Cate observed. 'Does this mean she won't be staying long?'

'More clothes can always be bought if need be,' he murmured, refusing to accept any limitation where Rosalie James was concerned.

She was here.

The advantage was his.

He wasn't about to let it slip.

Rosalie was a mass of jangling nerves. She'd been reasonably calm on the flight, having made the decision to come and feel her way through whatever developed between Adam Cazell and herself. She had no idea whether it would be good for her or not, but she'd reasoned it would at least get rid of the torment of wondering. But the moment she'd emerged from the plane and saw him waiting for her, the sheer physical impact of the man had instantly assaulted her courage.

He emitted too much power.

It wasn't safe.

How was she going to control this...this experiment?

Would she feel free to walk away afterwards?

She tore her gaze from him and fastened it on his daughter—her lifeline out of trouble if she felt she couldn't go through with Rebel's advice to lay herself open to being a woman with Adam Cazell. Looking at Cate eased the panic in her mind.

The young teenager was wearing a cute outfit— white Capri pants and a white midriff top printed with red cherries, a quirky red hat jammed over her short dark waves. The wide grin on her face promised she was happy about Rosalie's visit, looking forward to sympathetic female company.

The flight attendant brought down the bag she'd repacked days ago in case she did decide to take up Adam Cazell's invitation after she'd finished the photo shoot in New York. It contained enough coordinating garments to cover a week on a Caribbean island, but now a week felt too long. A host of fearful *what ifs* crowded her mind as she thanked the attendant for his services and fought for the composure to face Adam Cazell with a smile. After all, she had come here of her own free will.

'Welcome to Tortola.'

His deep voice seemed to reverberate through her. The silver grey eyes simmered with pleasure as she took the offered hand and managed to say, 'Thank you. It all looks spectacularly beautiful from the air.'

'Our cove is especially pretty,' Cate leapt in. 'The water is a lovely emerald green and you can walk straight down to it from Dad's villa.'

'Sounds wonderful!' Rosalie enthused, thankful that Adam released her hand so she could take his daughter's. 'I don't think I need to ask how you are, Cate. You look like you've been having the time of your life.'

She laughed and squeezed Rosalie's hand as her eyes twinkled up at her father. 'I've been smartening Dad up on lots of things.'

'Didn't know I was so dim until she cut loose on me,' he rolled out with mock concern.

Cate punched his arm. 'I never said you were dim.'

He grinned at Rosalie. 'She shouldn't have told me why I always lost at *Scrabble*. I've won the last three games straight.' He picked up her suitcase and gestured towards the four-wheel drive jeep which was obviously their island transport. 'Let's get out of the sun before it fries our brains.'

She walked between the two of them, Cate dominating the conversation with her plan for the afternoon. Since it was already after midday, they'd drive along the coast to Road Town, stop at a restaurant on the harbour, have lunch, then perhaps stroll around the colourful Main Street shops if Rosalie felt like it before taking the Ridge Road over to Cane Garden Bay and along the coast again to where their villa was situated.

'I'm happy for you to take me anywhere on the island, Cate,' Rosalie promised her, pleased to find no sign of disgruntlement in the girl.

Perhaps Adam Cazell had spoken the truth when he'd said the invitation was as much from his daughter as it was from him. Certainly Cate didn't seem to be harbouring any resentment about losing out on a continued exclusive twosome with her father. In fact, she eagerly claimed most of Rosalie's attention, playing tourist guide as they drove to Road Town, chatting on about all they'd done here in the past month, asking about the photo shoot and other modelling engagements coming up in the near future.

For the most part Adam listened, adding the occasional comment but apparently content to let his daughter entertain their guest. It was the same at lunch—wonderful seafood accompanied by tropical fruit drinks—promoting the lazy, relaxed mood of being on holiday, nothing expected of her. The point was reached where she could look at the man who'd brought her here without feeling threatened by his overwhelming maleness.

He was good with Cate. Very good. The affectionate teasing between them reminded her of the ease she always felt with Zachary Lee—nothing hidden, complete understanding. Both of them big men. Was that part of why she found Adam Cazell so attractive physically? Enormous strength was probably linked in her subconscious mind to the ability to protect—a deeply rooted appeal for her. But strength had to be trusted, as well. It could hurt.

Still, she sensed no harm in him. An underlying purpose, waiting patiently for the right time—yes—but the realisation there was to be no haste about connecting more intimately with her made it easy to enjoy being a tourist for a while. And the shops Cate led them into after lunch had much of the unique local colour of the region to offer; fascinating handicrafts, some stunning art from watercolours to sculpture, wonderful island sundresses and shirts.

She even felt brave enough to tease Adam. 'So this is where you bought your gorgeous shirt.' It was printed with red and pink hibiscus flowers, teamed with white slacks.

He laughed. 'Goes with the territory.'

'Makes you look…slightly less formidable.'

'I don't want you to think of me as formidable at all.'

She shook her head. 'I don't believe clothes make the man.'

'Nor the woman,' he quickly returned, the silver bullet eyes shafting that point home, causing her heart to skip at the reminder that this was not just a superficial attraction between them. She sensed there was something innate in both of them tugging to be known, shared, experienced to the full.

It was right to have come, she decided.

Though it didn't make the journey with him any more predictable or less frightening. And Rosalie inwardly recoiled from the idea of giving all of herself. There were some places in her life she kept blocked off. Best that they remain so. The sharing with Adam Cazell could not cross that line. She wouldn't let it.

When they finally arrived at the villa, having driven over the central mountainous spine of the island to the other side, it became obvious that 'our cove' was precisely that, the whole area facing onto it owned by Adam, ensuring a private tropical paradise.

The villa itself was an amazing piece of architecture, a series of pavilions linked by walkways over artificial ponds and artfully designed gardens. There was an inviting array of open areas for viewing the beach and the glorious shades of the sea. The furniture was mostly made of cane, the furnishings all in bright cheerful colours. The whole place generated a sense of pleasurable relaxation.

She was introduced to a cook and three maids who came in daily to look after everything. Two gardeners in the grounds waved to her as Adam indicated she was his guest. Cate showed her to a spacious guest suite that provided her with every modern convenience. Luxury on a grand scale, she thought, yet none of it was an assault on the environment, more a harmonious fitting in to what was here. And no doubt the employment required from the local inhabitants was appreciated by them.

Did Adam Cazell pay them well? She hoped so. Any form of exploitation of native people was anathema to her. She would not model for any dress designer who employed cheap Chinese labour working in oppressive sweatshops. People were people all over the world, though far too often the country of their birth condemned them to a life that had more to do with survival than getting any pleasure from it.

The heat of the afternoon was alleviated by a breeze wafting from the sea. Large overhead fans circulated it more effectively. Rosalie unpacked, undressed, took a shower, then rested on the queen size bed, needing some quiet time to herself. She'd come a long way today. And she'd be going even further tonight...with Adam Cazell.

Best it be done quickly, she told herself, and not think too much about it. She didn't want him thinking too much, either, trying to draw more from her than she was willing to reveal. Her own lack of sexual experience wouldn't matter. The driving force would come from him. All she had to do was surrender to the feelings he stirred, ride them instead of holding back...just let it happen.

A knock on the door woke her. 'It's getting on for dinner time, Ms. James,' a voice called out, the West Indian timbre of it denoting one of the maids. 'Will you be joining Mr. Cazell and Miss Cate, or would you like something in your suite?'

'No. I'll join the others for dinner. Thank you,' she called back.

'We'll be serving it on the front verandah, Ms. James, at seven o'clock.'

'Thank you.'

The light was considerably less brighter now. Must be close to sunset, Rosalie thought, hurrying so as not to miss it from the verandah overlooking the cove. She'd already planned what to wear. Designed for seduction, she thought ironically, knowing no seduction was required. But the outfit did signal her willingness to enter a sexual relationship. She had no doubt Adam Cazell was adept at reading such signals.

A nervous little shiver ran down her spine as she fastened the sarong skirt around her waist. No panties. She might baulk at undressing, the sheer vulnerability of being uncovered striking too many frightening chords. The faster this deed was done, the less she would have to keep her courage steadfast.

The matching top was gathered into a halter neckline and tied at the back. No bra. The filmy material, printed in soft greens and browns, was lined with a flesh coloured fabric. Her nakedness underneath it was not obvious, but accessibility was. It felt strange, knowing she'd be acting on what the clothes promised. Always before they'd been just clothes draped on her body.

She brushed her hair and left it falling loose down

her almost bare back. Some pink-brown lipstick to accentuate her mouth, a touch of green to lend depth to her eyes, and her make-up was done. She slipped her feet into minimal sandals, one strap decorated with green and amber glass beads.

Her pulse quickened as she left her private suite and took the walkway to the main living areas. This was a journey that had to be taken, she kept telling herself. As Rebel said, she was a woman, and there was no denying Adam Cazell had awakened a sexuality that was suddenly craving a sense of fulfilment. Fear had to be suppressed. Her whole adult life had been aimed at helping children who desperately needed help. Now…tonight…she was determined on doing something for herself.

Right or wrong…she would do it…and deal with afterwards…afterwards.

Adam stood near the edge of the verandah, watching the changing shades of colour in sky and sea as the sun started dipping below the horizon. He was also harnessing enough discipline to play the relaxed host this evening, not giving Rosalie any cause to shy away from him. If he could get her to stay in his company after Cate left them, he'd know she was willing to try a relationship with him. It was essential to move slowly, win ground bit by bit, assume nothing.

'I led Rosalie into the best shop for clothes,' Cate remarked, 'but she wasn't interested in buying any.'

He turned to smile ruefully at his over-keen daughter who was seated at the table, flipping through the magazine she'd bought in town. 'That's not why she's here,' he said matter-of-factly.

'Well, she's not all over you like a rash, Dad,' came the pertinent observation.

'We agreed that Rosalie James was different, Cate,' he reminded her.

She frowned. 'I think you're being too laid back. If you want her to be your girlfriend, she has to know it.'

'She knows it. It's a matter of her *choosing*. And I have to respect that or she'll be flying out of here.'

It felt odd to be discussing the situation with his thirteen-year-old daughter, yet he liked the understanding they were forging, the honesty between them. He actually felt less alone, as he knew she did, as well. The trick was to gather Rosalie James into their togetherness, make her feel at home with them.

'People can be persuaded into choices,' Cate pointed out with a wise look.

'If they want to be,' he cautioned.

'She wouldn't have come if she didn't *want* to be. I'll disappear after dinner. Watch cable TV in my bedroom. You might not have bags of time, you know. I think you'd better start persuading.'

'I appreciate your thoughtfulness,'

Her grin acknowledged the calculation behind it. 'All in a good cause.'

She went back to perusing the magazine, just as

Adam spotted Rosalie coming along the walkway from the guest wing. The sight of her took his breath away. She moved like an island girl; loose-limbed, hips swaying, subtly flaunting her femininity yet with a grace that seemed entirely natural. Her long hair swayed too, a shiny curtain of black silk falling to her waist.

But for the creamy colour of her skin, she looked like an island girl, dark hair, dark eyes, exotically dressed in a sarong-style skirt with a halter top that seemed to shift to the movement of breasts that were free of any constriction. The greens and browns of the soft fabric projected a sensual earthiness.

This was not the angel of Phnom Penh. Nor the regal presence at the opera. This was the woman she meant to be here.

Tonight!

Adam's heart started rocketing around his chest.

No persuasion needed.

Though he instantly realised the clock on this visit was ticking down even faster than he had anticipated and somehow...every muscle in his groin was tightening...somehow he had to gain a longer hold on her—a strong hold so she couldn't slip away from him.

Rosalie James had decided.

But the end game had to be his.

CHAPTER SEVEN

THE table was cleared apart from a large platter containing a variety of cheeses, crackers and slices of tropical fruit to be idly picked at whenever tempted. Cate had gone to her room to watch some television program she liked. The maids had been dismissed for the night. Rosalie and Adam were finally alone together, sipping from small glasses of Tokay which seemed to complement the rich balminess of the evening.

An almost full moon, a host of bright stars in the sky, the sound of the sea booming onto an outer reef, flares spotlighting the tropical garden, seductive food and wine, absolute privacy...nothing could be more romantic, Rosalie thought appreciatively, the mixture of primitive splendour and sophisticated luxury appealing to all the senses. Certainly it lulled her nervous fear over what was to come. Which, of course, had been Adam Cazell's design.

He looked sexy, too, his loose, collar-less, gauzy white shirt fastened only by a couple of buttons at the front, the breadth of his muscular shoulders and chest very visible. His white cotton trousers had a drawstring waistline—provocatively casual. One tug...the flick of a thumb on those two buttons...

81

Rosalie took a deep breath and wrenched her mind off thinking how he might look completely nude. 'Do you come here often, Adam?' she asked.

He shrugged. 'Whenever I feel like a break from the merry-go-round of business and people. I've found it the perfect place to unwind and shed pressures.'

'Is it your favourite place?'

A whimsical smile. 'For what it offers, yes. But other places provide different pleasures. I'm a traveller, Rosalie. Like you.' His eyes pinned hers, silently punctuating the similarity, tugging on that chord in her heart that responded to him, insidiously suggesting there was more to this attraction than sexual chemistry.

It meant nothing, she swiftly told herself, and made the point, 'I don't travel for pleasure, Adam.'

'I know,' he said softly. 'You travel for people. What were you doing in Thailand?'

She frowned, wondering how much he knew about her work with children. He'd seen her with the choir of orphans in Phnom Penh. Was there any harm in telling him more?

'You told Cate over dinner that you'd been there recently,' he reminded her.

'I was visiting my brother, Joseph. He runs a school for orphans in Bangkok. Joseph was one himself before our parents adopted him.'

'Joseph from Thailand, Zuang Chi from China, Rebel, the English one, Zachary Lee from America...

tell me the others in this remarkable family of yours. Rebel mentioned there were fourteen of you and Celeste said you came from all over the world.'

It was a natural enough curiosity, given that he already knew of the family, yet Rosalie knew he was homing in on her—who she was, where she had come from. What would he make of her origin if she revealed that to him? She felt reluctant to give up anything that was intensely private to her, yet she was proud of the James family and how the lives of so many children had been turned around, demonstrating how love and the right care could nurture such wonderfully positive outcomes.

'Tiffany Makana is from Fiji. Tiffany is the only one of us who was a baby when adopted. She was left on a church doorstep. Carol Tay was the oldest one adopted. She and her son, Alan, came from Vietnam. Suzanne Griffith is from Canada. Tom is a native Australian, an aborigine. All of them and Zachary Lee are settled in Australia.'

'That's nine accounted for,' Adam prompted.

'Muhammad and Leah are from India. Both of them are back there now. Muhammad is a doctor and Leah is a nurse, working in Calcutta. Shasti is from Ethiopia. She's in Africa, working for Unicef. Kim came from Korea and is now based in Hong Kong.'

'And you?'

'I was brought out of the Philippines.'

'But you're not a native of that country,' he said with certainty.

'I was born there. My mother was half Filippino, half American.'

'Your father?'

She shrugged. 'I don't know his heritage. I do know he was stationed at a U.S. base near Manila and he must have been tall.'

'You don't remember him?'

'No.'

'No photos?'

'They weren't married, Adam,' she said dryly. 'My mother was illegitimate and so was I. There was no family to take me in when she died.'

'How old were you then?'

'Seven.'

'You went into an orphanage?'

'There are many homeless children in the Philippines. I prefer not to talk about that part of my life.'

His eyes bored into hers, speculation simmering. She blocked it off by demanding knowledge of him. 'Tell me about your family.'

'There's only Cate. My parents are dead. I was an only child. I guess my background could be called privileged in the sense that I wanted for nothing and was sent to good schools.' His mouth quirked into a wry little smile. 'My parents were proud of me in a distant kind of way, but basically I was a cuckoo in their nest and they didn't know what to make of me.'

A cuckoo in the nest...a very evocative statement, recalling that moment by the lake at Davenport Hall when she'd sensed his aloneness. 'So you've climbed to the top of your mountain on your own,' she said, intrigued by the strength of will that had taken him there.

'I've had good people working with me. Just as you've had the James family to support what you want to do, Rosalie.' His eyes locked onto hers with meaningful purpose. 'But the drive comes from within, fuelled by needs that demand we keep going because there's no end to what can be achieved. Isn't that so?'

Her heart jiggled alarmingly as he linked them to a truth she couldn't deny. He was closing in on the person she was, moving to a level that had nothing to do with the sexual one she had accepted. Action was needed, prompting him into pursuing what she *was* offering.

'Perhaps that applies to me and my work with children. There are always more to be helped,' she conceded. 'But you, Adam, surely you could sit on your laurels now. What comes after a global airline?'

She rose from her chair, gesturing to the view as she moved to the edge of the verandah and looked out on the tropical night. 'You could simply enjoy this,' she tossed back at him.

'I do enjoy it. But it's not enough.' He pushed out of his chair and strolled slowly towards her. 'There is no *place* that would be enough. You don't even think of putting down roots, do you, Rosalie?'

'I was talking about you,' she quickly protested.

His eyes gleamed a mocking challenge. 'And I'm pointing out how alike we are. It doesn't matter how many places we leave our suitcases in. You live inside yourself, just as I do.'

'Everyone does that,' she argued, feeling he was weaving a net around her, inexorably coupling her with him.

'Most people get attached to things. Their country. Their community. Their home. Such things give meaning to their existence. Roots...'

He let the word linger, taunting her attempt to evade the links he was forging between them. Rosalie remained silent, every muscle in her body tensing at his nearness. He had to touch her soon. Any moment now. That was the prime reason for inviting her here, wasn't it? All this talking was confusing the issue.

He took her hand, engulfing it with the warmth and strength of his. 'Let's go for a walk together.'

A walk?

He drew her off the verandah and onto the path that led down to the beach before Rosalie found wits enough to query his purpose. 'This is not what I expected from you,' she blurted out.

'Something wrong with a friendly walk?' he lilted at her.

'We aren't...friends.' She shot him a heated look, intensely aware of the physical link of their hands and knowing—*knowing*—there'd been a sexual current running between them all through dinner. 'Don't pretend it's friendship you want from me, Adam.'

'Lovers can also be friends, Rosalie. Especially when they have much in common.'

'Are you friends with all your previous lovers?'

'There've been none like you.'

'Oh, come on!' she protested, savagely dismissing the hook he was throwing out before it sank in and affected her. 'You've probably said that to all of them. And why not? Everyone's different. But don't expect me to believe it means something special.'

'So you use my playboy reputation against me to deride my sincerity,' he mocked. 'It doesn't change what I feel with you, Rosalie. And it is unique in my experience.'

'Fine!' she clipped out, impatient with flattery, with charm, with anything he used to delay the inevitable.

'Why are you so determined to deny it?'

She tried to quell the turbulence he stirred inside her, tried to think straight. 'It won't change anything, Adam. And I wish you'd stop trying to tie me to you in some way.' She halted, stubbornly refusing to be led down paths she was not prepared to take. 'This is a mistake. I'm going back.'

Before she could begin her retreat he stepped in front of her, wheeling to face her, lifting her hand to his shoulder, leaving it there to wind his arms around her in an imprisoning embrace.

'You think sex will make it go away, Rosalie?' he challenged, his eyes glittering with a ferocity of feeling that wrapped around her heart and squeezed it unmercifully. 'Is that why you came? Expecting to burn it off with a brief encounter?'

Her mind screamed yes, yet somehow he shamed her into seeking other answers, ending up in helpless confusion. And there was the heat of his body seeping into hers, arousing an acute awareness of the hard muscularity of his chest, his thighs, and the powerful aggression that demanded she surrender to it. She couldn't think. A flood of strange feelings were swamping her.

'You couldn't be more wrong, thinking the wanting is only physical,' he fiercely asserted. 'But let's test it, shall we? See how forgettable I am for you?'

She could only stare at him, too churned up to say anything. He lifted a hand to her face, his thumb tilting her chin, fingers dragging at the skin on her cheek as though wanting to claw through it to her inner self. His eyes blazed into hers, torches searing her soul, behind them a marauding will, determined on finding all that was hidden to him. A tremor shook her entire body as his mouth descended on hers.

Would he draw her secrets from her?

Would she ever be herself again?

Too late to reject him now. Too late...

He attacked with passion, forcing her lips apart, invading so quickly and with such explosive sensation, Rosalie was too stunned by the wild storm of response rushing through her to do anything but succumb to it. She clung to him, her hands instinctively linking behind his neck, holding on as he kissed her again and again, a tempestuous onslaught that was incredibly exciting.

Adam's head was spinning with the compelling urge to take her, have her. His body was raging with the need to do it now. But he knew it was what she wanted—over and done with—and he fought his own craving, instinctively clutching at the greater need to implant himself so deeply in her consciousness, he would always hold a place there. Be damned if he would let her root him out!

He wrenched his mouth from hers and took a long deep breath. Her eyes opened, unfocused, swimming as though she was caught in a whirlpool and the current was stronger than she had believed it could be. Adam was instantly reminded of the vulnerability he had sensed earlier today. Was this her first time? Had she never known passion with a man?

What should he do? What would be best for her? Ride the tide while she was still caught up in it or slow it down to a pace where she would be conscious of every move escalating to another level and another. Speed could shut fear out, but what memory of it would she have afterwards?

He had to make the memory stick. A blur was no good to him. He dropped a softer kiss on her mouth, his lips grazing sensually over hers, his tongue gliding teasingly over the sensitive inner tissues. He felt a convulsive little shiver run down her spine, her breasts lift and fall in a silent sigh.

'Walk with me, Rosalie,' he commanded, though his voice was no more than a gentle murmur.

She made no reply but there was no resistance in her body as he tucked her close to him, the silk river of her hair flowing over the arm he held around her waist. She leaned into his support as they walked and he knew she was shaken, unsure of where they were going but trusting his lead, accepting that what had been started was to be finished where he chose.

It didn't matter to her but it did to him. A night to remember, he kept telling himself, steering her across the lawn to where a flowering frangipani tree lent its exotic scent to the night air. Under its leafy branches were two sun-loungers facing the sea, but he didn't want to use them, not for making love to this woman. He moved her out of the shade, into the moonlight, close to the beach, where the floral scent mixed with the fresh salty smell of the sea and they could see the waves lapping the sand and the stars shining brightly above the horizon.

It felt right…a primitive setting for a primal act… his senses acutely alert to the fundamental nature of what had to be achieved here…a union that would bind her to him so deeply it could span the inevitable separations and endure in a space of its own.

He didn't question the need that centred exclusively on this woman. He trusted the gut instinct that told him unequivocally she was worth more than all the rest, and if he lost her, there would be an emptiness in his life that could never be filled. It flashed into his mind that there was one bond that would seal a future togetherness—a bond that he suddenly wanted so much it spilled into speech.

'Have you ever thought of having a child of your own, Rosalie?'

A child of her own...

Rosalie's stomach clenched at this further diversion from what she needed to happen. Her mind had been swirling with the sense of time and place—him at the centre of it—the tremulous feeling of being drawn into a web of natural forces that belonged to this moment, making it feel right for her to accept they were part of it, merging with it.

'There are too many children,' she cried in protest, the child she'd been too indelible a memory for her to see beyond it.

'Perhaps so,' he murmured, turning them both to face each other, his hands on her waist, his eyes focused intently on hers. 'Yet why deny what is natural to you...natural to *us?*' he went on, his deep voice resonating with a seductive power that vibrated through her. 'The sea, the earth, the air...you can smell it all around you, the birth and growth and recycling of life.'

'But we can choose what we do,' she broke in, and in a wild demonstration of the choice she had made, she reached out and deliberately undid the buttons on his shirt, baring his chest, placing her palms on the taut hot flesh underneath the flimsy fabric.

'Yes,' he agreed, scooping in a quick breath, his eyes glittering at the daring move. 'And I'll take the chance you've given me.'

There was none, she thought fiercely. She was *safe* from any *chance* happening tonight. If he was saying he wasn't about to use protection, it didn't matter. She didn't need it. Her fertile cycle was five days away. A new life would not be seeded on Tortola. She would be gone before any danger of pregnancy could occur. But she wouldn't tell him this. Let him think whatever he wanted as long as...

Her breath was trapped in her chest as his hands undid the ties at the back of her halter top. The bodice fell forward, leaving her breasts naked, their tip-tilted peaks tightening at the sudden exposure to the night air and his burning gaze.

In all her parading down the catwalk in see-through creations, she had never felt self-conscious about displaying her body. It simply showed off every aspect of how the clothes looked. But this was different. It was personal. And she could feel her flesh tingling with pinpricks of heat as he seemed to examine every contour, circles within circles.

Her breath finally whooshed from her lungs as he tossed the garment on the grass and stripped off his shirt, letting it fall behind him. His muscular strength was immediately evident, causing a little shiver of apprehension to run down her spine. He was such a big man. Would he be gentle with her?

Too late to worry about that now.

He had the physical fitness of a long-term survivor, and the build to support it. The mind, too—sharp, clever, far ranging. If she were to have a child by him...no, don't think it. Don't go there! Being with him like this was a giant step for her. Everything inside her quivered as he pulled the drawstring on his pants and stepped out of this clothing, fully naked and so aggressively male, fear instantly seized her mind.

She fought it. She had come here to know what it was like. Decision made. He was her choice. She forced her hands to undo the sarong, toss it aside with a bravado she didn't feel. His gaze raked her from head to foot and back again, a visual assault that had every muscle in her body clenching.

'The perfectly constructed woman,' he said with a wisp of a smile. 'No doubt you've been told that innumerable times. But you weren't made for strutting clothes. That's an artificial thing. Totally meaningless.'

He moved closer. Her heart broke into a wild fluttering as he ran his fingers lightly over her shoulders, down her arms. He lifted her hands to his shoulders, then traced her underarms with the same tantalising brush of his fingertips, the feather-light caress continuing down to her waist, her hips, thighs, raising trails of prickling heat as though his touch was infiltrating her bloodstream and it was responding with eager leaps and bounds.

'This body was made to mate with a man,' he murmured, his gaze holding hers with mesmerising intensity. His hands spread over her stomach and glided up to cup her breasts. 'And these were made to suckle a child.' His thumbs fanned her hardened nipples, making them ache for a more satisfying contact. 'This is what life is about, Rosalie...our coming together just as nature intended.'

She savagely blocked that claim out of her mind. This was nothing but a physical connection and she wouldn't let it be turned into more. His arms pulled her into an embrace that sent shockwaves of sensation from every point of contact. This was it, she thought in a frenzied flow of fear and excitement.

'Come with me,' he commanded, his voice suddenly harsh with an urgency he carried into a kiss that seemed violently invasive, yet instantly stirring a fierce passion to commit herself to an equal plundering of his mouth, silencing all the talk, wanting only action.

But he spoke anyway, silently, insidiously reaching into the woman he said she was, lifting her up, her long hair coiled around his hand, arching her back so that he could take her breasts in his mouth, one by one, swirling his clever, knowing tongue around her nipples, kissing them with a deep rhythmic tug that sent arcs of piercing pleasure through her body... terrible, wonderful pleasure that awoke every long-suppressed female instinct inside her, bringing them to screaming wanton life.

Then he laid her on the soft grass and trailed kisses across her stomach as though wooing the woman within, or warming the womb into which he'd spill his seed, and his hands were easing the passage to it, caressing her inner thighs, parting the intimate folds of her sex, promising what was to come with softly sliding fingers.

And her body was craving it, convulsively welcoming each subtly tantalising invasion. But her inner focus changed, became confused as he moved his mouth lower and found a far more intensely sexual target, generating waves of exquisitely excruciating pleasure that she could hardly bear.

She felt herself writhing, arching, her whole body violently out of control. Her hands were scrabbling through his hair, pulling, pressing, blindly seeking some course that would answer the tumultuous need within. And finally he answered it, lifting himself over her, knowing she was open to him, open and waiting tremulously, wanting the ultimate fulfilment of all he could give her, and she sighed with intense relief as she felt him push into her, felt her inner muscles contract around him, felt the glorious fullness moving slowly onward, meeting the resistance of her virginity, pausing.

Even in that brief moment of panic she couldn't bear the thought of him stopping. If there was pain, there was pain. She didn't care. She dug her fingernails into his back, crying out, 'Do it! Do it!' the savage urgency of her desire for him to finish what he'd started overriding any hesitation by either of them.

He surged through the thin barrier—only the slightest sense of tearing, swiftly soothed by the fierce satisfaction of feeling him move past it, going deeper, deeper, filling the empty ache, replacing it with an ecstatic sense of completion.

It didn't hurt. They fitted. And he drove that amazing knowledge into her consciousness again and again, slowly, quickly, a wildly addictive rhythmic beat, mating with her, she thought on a sharp wave of new understanding, and she was helpless to do anything but take him into herself, discovering dark untravelled roads of emotion, deep inner needs clawing at the closed gates in her mind, forcing them open, exulting in being open to him and whatever he forged with her, climbing for an endless time, reaching a taut agony of pleasure, a piercing, awesome place that burst into incredibly sweet ripples that released a swift, brilliant sense of melting together, merging...

And as she lay enthralled by the changes he'd wrought in her by this act of mating, still held by him, she could not stop herself from wondering about the new life they might have made if it had been the right time, and felt a desire for it she would never have conceded before.

The absolute completion, she thought, and realised for the first time, what Rebel meant about being a woman…with a man who made her feel she wanted all this with him…all there could be between them… because of how it felt together.

And none of it—none of it—was forgettable.

CHAPTER EIGHT

ADAM didn't want to think. He just wanted to hold on to her, fill his senses with everything about her, her warm musky scent, the satin smoothness of her skin, the silky spill of her hair, the soft rise and fall of her breasts on his chest as she breathed her contentment to be with him like this, her head on his shoulder, their legs in an intimate splice.

Yet thoughts kept darting in and out of his mind, all of them related to her choosing him to take her virginity. How big a thing was that? Had she simply decided it was time and she could use him to do it? Have the experience he offered, no strings attached?

Everything she'd said tonight pointed to an acceptance of a brief encounter only. But was that defensive? Maybe she was afraid to feel too much. She was drawn to him, possibly against her will, fighting to reduce the attraction to dismissible limits. Did she realise now that some things were too strong to be rationalised away? What was she feeling this minute?

Her first time!

He hadn't even asked... 'Are you okay, Rosalie?' The words burst from his lips in jolting concern that he hadn't considered any physical distress. She'd pushed him, gone with him, but whether out of driven desire or determination…had the pleasure outweighed the pain? He knew she had climaxed.

Impatient for an answer, he rolled her onto her back and propped himself up to watch her face, read her expression. 'Why didn't you tell me it was your first time?'

She sighed, shook her head slightly, as though denying it, or denying it any importance, perhaps wishing he hadn't realised.

'Rosalie…' He gently stroked her cheek, forcing the dark liquid eyes to look directly into his. '…I'm not a fool.'

She took a deep breath and admitted, 'I didn't want it to change anything. I wanted you to take me as you would any other woman.'

'You're not any other woman.'

Her mouth quirked into a wry little smile. 'I've heard it said all cats are the same in the dark.'

'Only by people of no discrimination.'

'But it is the same…the same act.'

'No. It's different with every person. It relates very closely to how you feel about them. It wasn't just chance that you chose me for this,' he said with sudden certainty.

She seemed to struggle for a reply. 'Rebel said… I'd be safe with you.'

'Safe…' It was a strange word to use, so strange Adam knew intuitively it was important, possibly a key to all her reactions to him. He filed it away in his mind, plus the fact that she had discussed her decision with her sister, revealing her sense of vulnerability about it.

'Did I hurt you, Rosalie?' he asked softly, feeling a wave of tenderness as he comprehended the bravery that had brought her this far with him.

'No. It was…' Her face broke into a brilliant smile. '…amazing, Adam.'

The way she spoke his name gave him an enormous thrill. It felt like an acknowledgment of him as someone very special. Her first lover. Her *only* lover, he fiercely vowed.

'Thank you,' she added huskily, reaching up to stroke his cheek. 'It was more…than I'd ever allowed it could be.'

And would be more still, Adam determined, recognising an awed wonderment in her touch, in her voice, in her eyes. But he had to take care of this beginning first, wash away any blood, ease any sense of rawness, make her want him again. And again. Her 'Thank you' was warning enough there was a clock ticking in her head and it had to be stopped.

He rose to his feet and drew her up with him. 'Let's walk on down to the sea,' he said, wrapping his hand around hers and leading off, aware that the docility emanating from her now might soon be gone. He had to seize every advantage she surrendered to him.

Rosalie could hardly believe she was doing this… walking naked with a man who was equally naked. It was strangely liberating, as though everything else in their lives had been shucked off and there were only the two of them in a world of their own. Like Adam and Eve. She smiled at the whimsical thought. Could the Garden of Eden have been like this?

She looked up at the stars, felt the granules of sand crunching under her feet and a gentle breeze wafting over her skin, smelled the salt from the sea and the scent of exotic blooms, and revelled in a sense of unspoiled innocence, a clean sheet upon which anything could be written, a shiny new beginning.

My birth as a woman, she thought, glancing at the man who had brought her here, wondering if he had knowingly set this scene for her, aware of its magical appeal and sensitive to how it would feel.

He caught her glance. 'Yes?'

But she already knew the answer, remembering what he'd spoken of beforehand, words she hadn't wanted to hear. 'It's a fantasy,' she said in a rush of understanding how clever he was.

'No. It's real. Everything around us...you...me... it's all real, Rosalie.' His smile was very white in the moonlight. 'Why not just live the moment?'

So seductive...living the moment. They walked into a softly dying wave that frothed around her feet. There was only a gentle swell in the bay. She could hear the boom of the sea breaking on the reef beyond it. His hand tightened around hers as they moved on, though there was no danger of her falling or being swept away from him. The water was like a warm caress on her legs, the sand underfoot quite firm.

Sight, sound, smell, touch…easy to immerse herself in these physical realities, easy to accept their influence on her emotions. Let go of everything else, she told herself, and just be a woman with a man for this one night, *live the moment*—a magical moment in time—without any reference to the past or future.

She'd been conscious of a stickiness between her thighs but whatever it was—some bleeding, a residue of their sexual intimacy—the water washed it away. Adam saw her touching herself there and halted, his face flashing concern.

'Are you sore?'

She laughed away a wave of shyness at his sharp observation. 'I said it was amazing, Adam. I wasn't expecting…what you did.'

He grinned, relieved to think she was remembering the pleasure he'd given her. 'There are many other things I'd like to do with you,' he said wickedly.

'I want to swim.' She wriggled her fingers against his grasp, reacting to a sudden sense of entrapment, a feeling he wasn't going to let her go.

He did, instantly releasing her hand. 'Then we'll swim together.'

She didn't mind that idea.

Sharing was fine.

Imprisonment was not.

They were already waist-deep and they both dove forward, swimming towards the centre of the bay,

Adam matching his pace to hers. It was invigorating and blissful, feeling the water streaming past her naked body, her hair floating completely weightless.

She'd never done this before...another first... imbuing her with an even deeper sense of being at one with totally primitive elements, free of all care from the strictures of society and the career that demanded perfect grooming.

She grinned at the thought of seaweed hair horrifying the designers who employed her, and the photographers with their finicky vision of perfection.

'What's amusing you?' Adam asked.

They'd slid into a lazy sidestroke and he was watching her, perhaps checking if she was tiring. She stopped swimming and trod water, curious to know how he viewed her. Was the glamour she portrayed as a model part of her attraction for him?

'This is not the woman you saw at the opera in New York,' she stated provocatively.

He grinned. 'I like it better with your armour off.'

She cocked her head, considering his answer. 'More...touchable?'

'More reachable.'

With a quick manouvre, he took her hands and linked them behind his neck, then kicked out underneath her, bringing her buoyant body up to float above his as he started a slow backstroke, taking her with him towards the beach.

'I don't need to be towed,' she told him, though she didn't mind. In fact, it made her feel happily aware of how strong he was, and using that strength to give her an easy ride through the water.

'Just keeping you safe,' he answered.

Safe...

Physically she did feel safe with him now. The fear she'd attached to having any sexual activity was gone. He'd shown her how incredibly marvellous it could be with the right man, a man who knew how to give pleasure instead of...her mind shied away from the brutal activities she'd seen as a child.

It need not be like that.

It should not be like that.

Zachary Lee had told her, assured her, but right up until this night with Adam the barrier of fear had held back any real belief in what anyone had said. Even now it seemed strange that she could feel this big man moving beneath her, his naked sex rolling over her stomach as he swam, and not find it the least bit scary.

She liked it. Liked the brush of her breasts against his chest, too. And the drift of her thighs touching his. It was...deliciously sensual.

He stopped swimming. 'We can stand here,' he said, proving it by whooshing upright.

Her legs immediately sank, her feet hitting his, already firmly planted on the sandy bed. The surface of the water lapped her shoulders. Her arms instinctively lifted higher, winding themselves around his neck for support. Or maybe clinging on to the closeness because it felt so good.

Adam smiled at her. 'They called you an angel in

Phnom Penh. You looked like a queen in New York. Right now you sparkle like some mythical siren from the sea.'

'Luring men to their deaths?'

He laughed. 'Give me the kiss of life instead.'

She stared at his mouth, thinking she had never initiated a kiss. Except for kisses of greeting or affection, strictly on the cheek. He bent his head to make it easy for her lips to meet his, prompting the urge to experiment, to do it slowly, knowingly, assessingly, so she would remember exactly how it was and what she felt from it.

'Then let me do the kissing,' she said, her gaze flicking up to his in appeal, not wanting him to take control this time.

'As you wish,' he murmured, his eyes gleaming with a soft indulgence that sent a wave of warmth racing through her.

She touched her lips to his, a light rubbing that produced an electric tingling. Her tongue automatically licked out to soothe the effect and tasted salt, obviously from the sea water. His lips parted as she licked further, and tentatively she slid her tongue into the seductive heat of his mouth, moving it over his palate, a gentle, teasing invasion that felt daringly exciting. And slowly, his tongue began to tango with hers, inciting her into quick, darting movements that felt like a spurting fountain of delicious sensation.

Her heart quickened its beat, seeming to thunder in her ears, throb in her temples. Her head swam with a kind of intoxicating pleasure. One of her hands raked through his hair, curling around his scalp to grasp him more tightly to her. She felt his hands curve around her bottom, hoisting her higher so that their faces were level. She had to break the kiss to gulp in air.

'Wrap your legs around my hips, Rosalie,' he whispered urgently.

Yes, that was better. Very satisfying. And he was kissing her now, but she didn't mind him taking over because he knew how to make it even more exciting. Then she felt the insertion of himself between her thighs and gasped in shock that he could think of doing it in the water.

'Is this okay with you?' he quickly asked.

She looked at him, saw that he cared for her, and felt a wild elation at merging so intimately with him here. 'Yes,' she almost sang, throwing her head back and laughing at the stars in the brilliant night sky.

He pressed a trail of kisses down her long neck, found the pulse at the base of her throat and heated her blood with sizzling excitement as he plunged himself deep inside her, jolting her again with the incredible pleasure of feeling him there. And she tightened the lock of her legs around him, exulting in the sense of having this man in her hold, enveloping him, owning him.

Always she'd thought men had the power, power she had to skirt or somehow turn to her own use when possible, evade when it threatened her, but the realisation burst like a thunderclap that there was a different truth, especially with sex…the power of a woman to take a man like this, have him inside her because that was what she wanted and where he wanted to be. And it felt good. It felt great.

She swayed from side to side, loving the sensation of him being so deeply implanted within her. Then he moved her into a rocking motion that was even more delicious. And she kissed him with a spontaneity that just welled up in her and spilled into a joyous, uninhibited passion to experience all this wonderful man could give her, teach her, show her.

They stayed entwined like that for a long time, stoking the intense pleasure of being so intimately connected, revelling in it, savouring it, finally driving it to that shattering peak beyond which they fell into a blissful languor, content to simply feel the water floating around them.

Adam carried her out of it, her head resting contentedly on his shoulder. He carried her right up the beach to the villa garden and laid her on a lounger under a tree, lifting her long wet hair over the back rest to let it dry.

He broke off a large spray of creamy flowers from the tree and stretched out on the adjacent lounger, turning on his side to face her, smiling as he plucked the flowers from the spray and rubbed them gently over her skin, wiping away all the droplets of water and leaving the sweet scent of frangipani from the satin-soft petals.

Impulsively she took what remained of the spray

to do the same to him, pushing him onto his back and commanding him to lie still. She found it quite entrancing, touching him like this, tracing the delineation of his muscles, his magnificent physique completely bared to her wanderings over it.

She even caressed his inner thighs and the sexual components that had previously struck fear in her. No fear now. More a tender curiosity, and an awe in the masculinity that stirred so much that was female in her.

'Keep doing that and you'll arouse me again,' Adam growled.

She flashed him a teasing smile. 'Perhaps I want to see.'

'Then you make love to me, Rosalie,' he gruffly invited.

Make love?

How did one make love to a man?

She remembered what he'd done in giving intense pleasure to her, and not knowing if it would be at all the same for him, she twirled a flower over one of his nipples, then leaned over and drew the small nub into her mouth, copying his kiss and caresses.

She heard his sharply indrawn breath, felt the quick rise of tension in his body and felt a burst of elation in her success. Instinctively her hand glided down his stomach to stroke him as he'd stroked her, and she found it intensely exciting to feel him strengthening to full arousal under her touch.

She moved to his other nipple, tugging, licking,

thrilled by his response as she felt the hardness grow tighter, tighter, yet the skin at the top remained soft and clearly very sensitive for when she rolled her thumb over it, Adam's breathing became very quick and shallow. Then she remembered the terribly intimate kissing that had felt so incredibly exquisite and she moved down to take him in her mouth and…

She'd barely done so when Adam jackknifed up from the lounger, lifting her to straddle him, positioning them both so she sank onto his erection, and once again knew the fantastic feeling of taking him inside her. She slid forward, propping her hands on his shoulders, and found a rhythm of her own, which he made more intensely exciting by stroking her breasts, her stomach, her hips, wonderful circling caresses that sensitised her whole body, turning her into a wantonly sensual creature that gloried in every touch and movement.

And she could see the pleasure in his eyes, feel it coursing through his body, knew he felt all that she felt, and when they'd both driven it to exhilarating heights and finally brought it down to a gloriously humming contentment, she lay encompassed in his arms, dreamily looking up at a faraway heaven and knew what people meant when they spoke of heaven on earth.

It could not be better than this.

Complete and utter peace and happiness.

CHAPTER NINE

CATE had already started breakfast when Adam strolled out to the verandah where they invariably ate their meals. One of the maids had told him Miss James had not yet emerged from the guest suite. He had wanted Rosalie to share his bed but she had refused, insisting on sleeping alone in her own quarters. Which made him wonder if she was intent on filing last night away as a *fantasy*.

He shook his head over that damned insidious word, wishing she hadn't used it. Surely he'd given her enough effective reality to show her what they could have together in a continuing relationship. Yet still she had chosen to separate from him. The reason for it kept exercising his mind.

Because that was her unshakable intention—a brief connection, then separation? Or because she simply wasn't used to sleeping with a man, waking up to him, facing him the morning after?

He felt very much on edge until he could see her again and assess the outcome of their intimacy.

'Hi, Dad!'

He forced a smile for his daughter who was subjecting him to a blast of bright curiosity.

110

'So is it a good morning or not?' she pounced before he could even return her greeting.

'Looks good to me,' he drawled, viewing the sparkling water of the bay.

'I'm not talking about the weather,' Cate shot at him in exasperation. 'I *was* expecting to see you and Rosalie come to breakfast together.'

He shrugged. 'Possibly she's still asleep.'

'You don't *know?*'

'I don't think she'd appreciate my going to her suite to check,' he answered dryly.

Cate huffed and shook her head knowingly at him. 'You must be slipping, Dad. I thought for sure it was on last night.'

He frowned at her rather crass view of his relationships with women, though he couldn't deny sex had been the driving force behind most of them. Certainly there'd never been a case of separate bedrooms under the same roof before.

'I did tell you Rosalie was different, Cate,' he said shortly, moving to pour himself a glass of pineapple juice.

A worried look gathered on her brow. 'She didn't actually turn you down, did she? I mean…you've still got a chance with her?'

'First and foremost Rosalie James is our guest. We'll *all* do what she wants.'

It was a curt reproval, possibly unfair given his daughter's personal interest in this affair, but he didn't want to discuss the situation with her, especially when he didn't have a firm handle on it himself.

He settled in his usual chair at the table and sipped the juice. Cate attacked her bowl of cereal again, her discontent over his failure to win the woman of her choice clouding her face. It reflected his own discontent. Not that he was about to concede failure. Rosalie had certainly been happy having sex with him—one very positive factor—but the parting had rattled his confidence in sealing a deeper, more lasting bond.

'You can't always order what you want, Cate,' he wryly observed.

'But what can she have against you?' came the instant argument. 'You're rich. You could give her anything. You've got sort of macho good looks. And for an older guy, you're in great shape. Even the girls at school think you're sexy.'

'Sex isn't everything. Neither is wealth,' he sliced back, not liking her thinking in those terms. She was barely thirteen. Had he been a bad example to her? Or was this just the silly stuff young girls carried on about? 'Has your mother talked to you about boys?'

She huffed and glared derision at him. 'I'm not a baby, Dad.'

'No, but you do need to learn to place a value on yourself, and that has more to do with the person you are inside than what any boy has to offer in the way of sexiness or what he can buy you.'

She cogitated this for several moments, then asked,

'Is that the difference? The value Rosalie places on the person she is inside?'

'In the long run, yes,' he answered with certainty.

'But she did come. That means something, doesn't it?' She paused, then said hopefully, 'A trial run?'

'Perhaps,' he said non-committally, too acutely aware that the trial might have run its course last night if Rosalie's only aim was to experience sex with a man.

'So what do we do today? I could leave you together, cycle over to...'

'No. Let's just carry on normally. Okay?'

She grimaced. 'Won't give you many opportunities to be alone with her.'

He shook his head. 'I don't want you to feel pushed aside anymore. You and I, Cate...we're a team.'

Her eyes lit with delight in this further proof of his commitment to her and Adam realised anew how little time he had given her over the years. One summer vacation together didn't make up for it, and he wasn't about to erode what ground he had established with his daughter by concentrating entirely on Rosalie. Besides which, it would probably be the worst move he could make in her eyes, too. It was Cate's welfare that had spurred her into accepting his company in the first place.

'Well, I guess you know what you're doing, Dad,' she said happily, and with a shrug at his supposedly superior experience, she went back to eating her cereal.

The problem was, he didn't. He could only feel his way forward with Rosalie James. She didn't fit into any easy to categorise personality—still a mystery to him. He now knew she'd been born in the Philippines, of mixed parentage, orphaned at seven, and rescued from what he surmised to be wretched circumstances by some member of the James family.

She'd grown up in a caring, supportive household, climbed the modelling ladder to international stardom, used her earnings and all her spare time to help needy orphans, and up until last night, steered clear of any intimate relationship with a man.

Because she hadn't felt *safe* with them?

Sexually safe?

This would suggest some earlier traumatic experience, perhaps even as far back as when she was a homeless child. *I prefer not to talk about that part of my life.* Though she hadn't been raped. Her virginity repudiated any possibility of that.

Perhaps her talk of being *safe* with him related to trust.

Trust that he was an inherently decent person who wouldn't do anything to hurt her?

Trust that she could have sex with him without fear of any consequences she didn't want?

A playboy…

Except he wasn't playing with her. His priorities had been completely altered by Rosalie James. He was very, very serious about wanting her as a partner, not a temporary fling that barely touched his life. She had to be sensing that by now. But would she let herself respond to what they could have together, or was the determination—the need?—to be free and unencumbered completely unassailable?

The sound of footsteps instantly broke his private reverie and drew his gaze to the walkway from the guest house. His heart kicked with a buzz of aggressive adrenalin as he spotted Rosalie strolling towards the open living area that led out to the verandah.

She wore the same black and white polka dot skirt she had arrived in, the same sandals, a different white top—sleeveless and form-fitting, with a floppy frill gracing a V-neckline—but this latter garment did nothing to erase the ominous feeling that these were her travelling clothes.

Was she done with him? Satisfied that Cate was getting the parental attention she was missing before? Every muscle in Adam's body tensed in fighting mode. He would not accept a decision to leave, yet he couldn't force her to stay. He desperately needed a means of persuasion.

Rosalie's inner tension increased a hundredfold as Adam rose from the chair at the table on the verandah. He wore only a pair of white shorts which left so much of his physique bared to her view, it was impossible to push the memories of all her intimate contact with him into a manageable space in her mind. They flooded out, totally wrecking the discipline she had tried to impose upon the feelings he'd stirred in her.

Then he hit her with a smile that caused her heart to turn over—a smile reflecting *his* memory of the private sharing of themselves in a flash of pleasure that drove a tide of heat through her entire body.

'Good morning,' he said, while she struggled for the composure needed to deliver her decision to leave Tortola today.

The journey of discovery was over, she'd told herself in her private suite. Adam Cazell had done her a great favour in showing her there was another side to sex that held nothing negative at all. In fact, it was more wonderful than she could ever have imagined. But she had also realised it could become a terrible distraction if she let herself think about it too much. There were other more important things in her life than pursuing selfish pleasure.

'Hi!' came a greeting from Cate at the other end of the table, diverting Rosalie's attention to Adam's daughter who was also smiling pleasure in her presence. 'Sleep well?'

'Yes, thank you.'

She managed a responding smile even as she was struck by the realisation that she hadn't been considering how the girl might feel about an abruptly broken visit. Cate had put a lot into making her welcome yesterday, and the young teenager began pressing more hospitality onto her now.

'Dad hasn't eaten yet. I was just about to ask our

cook to get started on lashings of bacon and eggs. Would you like some, too?'

Rosalie hesitated, tempted by what would be a decadent breakfast for her. Modelling demanded she be always watchful of her weight but it was so long since she had indulged herself with such foods, she suddenly felt a strong yen for them.

'Could the eggs be poached?'

'Absolutely fat free,' Cate promised with a grin, and skipped off, heading for the kitchen.

'Juice?' Adam asked, moving to a sideboard where a jug of it sat beside a group of glasses. 'It's pineapple.'

'Lovely. Thank you,' she answered, totally in two minds about what she should do now. Disappointing Cate would not be good, though she did have her father with her.

'Cate is becoming very conscious of her figure. Terrified of developing puppy fat,' Adam remarked as he set the filled glass of juice on the table and pulled out a chair for her. 'The fashion industry has a lot to answer for,' he dryly added. 'I'm counting on you to give my daughter a balanced view of what is healthy eating. As a mere male, I'm not considered an authority on these important issues, but she'll listen to you.'

'Well, being overweight can become a blight on a girl's life,' Rosalie answered lightly, grateful for any line of conversation that excluded last night.

'On a boy's, too.' He settled back onto his own

chair, his eyes engaging hers as he pursued the topic. 'But it's mostly girls who go down the path of anorexia.'

Rosalie frowned over what was a very serious issue, indeed, and Adam's daughter was, as Rebel put it, in an *at risk* situation where she might be drawn to something she could control, something she thought might make her more attractive to the people whose opinion meant something to her, or simply draw more notice to herself.

'Are you concerned that Cate might fall victim to that kind of psychological problem?' she asked seriously.

'It's about control, isn't it? Right now I feel she's too controlled about what she eats. And too thin for her height.'

'She's at an age of quick growth. I'd call her more slender than thin, Adam. And I thought she ate with a normally healthy appetite yesterday.' But being so conscious of Adam, had she really noticed?

'No French fries with her fish at lunch. Which she picked at. And nibbled a bit of salad,' he informed her, demonstrating keen observation of his daughter's diet. 'Same last night. No sweets or cheese. A small bowl of bran flakes with skim milk for breakfast. She'll probably fiddle with a slice of melon while we eat ours.'

'It's not enough.'

'My thoughts exactly. Will you speak to her about it, Rosalie?'

She nodded, thinking how perverse it was that a girl who had every food available to her would choose to starve herself when there were so many starving children who'd fight over scraps from garbage bins.

'Have you told her mother, Adam?'

'I will. I've only noticed it since we've been here. But knowing Sarah, she'll only scold, not take the time to lay out a good pattern to follow. Cate admires you. Whatever you say is more likely to get through to her.'

'Okay. I'll try.'

'Thank you. After breakfast I usually go to my computer room to check on business for an hour or so. You won't mind if I leave you with her?'

She shook her head. 'Makes it easy for me to lead into it.'

He smiled, his eyes warming with very personal appreciation. 'I'm glad you're here, Rosalie. Everything about you feels good.'

She found herself smiling back, thinking the same of him, and not just in a sexual sense. He wasn't crowding her physically. Hadn't even touched her while seeing her seated. And this appeal for her help with Cate meant he both trusted and respected her as a friend to his daughter. And very possibly a needed friend.

Which reminded her that he'd linked Cate to his invitation to Tortola and she had seen that primarily as a subterfuge to get her here, perhaps wrongly so.

In fact, it was she who had pushed for and initiated what had happened last night. Adam might have intended talking about his daughter when he'd suggested the walk in the garden—a friendly walk. She'd only been thinking of herself and her need...to *use* him for what she wanted.

Shame curled through her as she recalled her claim they could only be lovers, not friends. And despite her emphatic dismissal of any other involvement, he had been a very generous and considerate lover to her. To leave both him and Cate flat now would be incredibly mean and wrong. She couldn't go today.

'I hope I can do some good,' she said with heartfelt sincerity.

'You have the power,' he returned with a wry twist, leaving her feeling he meant far more than any influence she could wield with his daughter.

'Bacon and eggs coming up in five minutes!' Cate announced, swinging attention back to her as she took her place at the table again. 'I told cook to do your bacon in the microwave, Rosalie. It should come out nice and crispy. No grease. One of the girls at school tipped us off on that trick.'

'Common practice in the U.S.,' Rosalie commented, smiling at her, then breaking straight into the subject of diet.

Adam sat back and let it all flow, feeling an intense sense of relief. Not for Cate's sake. It was true enough he was concerned about this dieting fad of hers, but it would have been easy enough to line up some expert nutritionist in London to set her straight on healthy eating. He thanked his lucky stars that he'd hit some sympathetic chord in Rosalie that had won more time from her.

She would stay today.

He watched her reaching out to Cate, projecting keen interest in the answers his daughter gave to questions about her friends at school, what kind of meals were served there, what they liked and disliked, how attuned the girls were to fashion and how much importance they placed on it. She was plumbing background information to give her an understanding of exactly where Cate was coming from, yet doing it in such a warm friendly way, Cate was basking in the personal attention.

And the simple truth was…Rosalie James cared.

There was no pretence in this.

She genuinely cared about his daughter.

Adam wondered what he had to do to draw the same caring to himself. Did he seem totally self-sufficient to her? Not in need of her company or craving to share more than a sexual connection?

I'm here, too, he thought, barely quelling a violent urge to impress that on her. He had to go slowly, use the time he'd won to put her in a comfort zone that made staying here more desirable than going. Whatever fears she had about associating with him any longer had to be erased, or at least soothed.

Tonight she would be his again.

Though his instincts warned him to let her think she was in control.

He smiled to himself. He didn't believe either of them were in control of the effect they had on each other. The difference was he wanted to explore it while she wanted to escape it. But the power of it was so strong…

And Rosalie had chosen to stay another night.

CHAPTER TEN

THE fourth night and the last night...

No going back on this decision, Rosalie told herself, though there was no absolute necessity for her to leave. She just felt herself getting in deeper and deeper with the Cazells. Their attractive company and the seductive ambience of the island seemed to be playing havoc with her usually strong sense of purpose.

She no longer had any *reason* for staying here and prolonging her visit was pure self-indulgence, which wasn't like her. Not like her at all. And it gave her an uneasy sense there'd be a price to be paid later— a bigger price every day she stayed. Nothing really came free. As it was, she wasn't sure how she was going to handle the attachment she now felt to both Adam and his daughter. She hadn't planned to get so involved with them, hadn't wanted either of them to tug at her heart.

She should have left after the first night.

Or at least the second.

Yet here they now were at Cappoon's Bay where a huge island party was being held around the Beach Shack, a ramshackle tin structure right in the surf. It was the night of the full moon and everyone was having a great time, eating, drinking, dancing to a metal band, living for the fun of the moment and certainly not thinking of tomorrow.

And the plain truth was, Rosalie couldn't remember ever feeling quite so relaxed and happy to do nothing, just being alive and enjoying it. She and Adam were sharing a rug on the sand, a hamper of drinks and snacks on hand for ready refreshment. Cate was in line for a Bomba dance further down the beach, joining in the hilarity and clapping of the closer spectators. It was another intoxicatingly beautiful night on Tortola.

But it had to be the last one. She had finally made an independent stand today and Adam had made the arrangements for her departure tomorrow, so it was counter-productive to start wishing the pleasure she'd known here could be stretched out indefinitely. Besides, Adam and Cate would be heading back to London themselves at the end of the week.

'Can't you stay until then?' Cate had pleaded.

'I'm expected in Paris to get ready for the pret-a-porter fashion shows,' Rosalie had excused, instinctively avoiding the extra intimacy of departing the island together, like a family going home from vacation.

They weren't a family. Yet there had been times when she'd felt a strong sense of belonging, especially with the man who was sitting beside her. It wasn't only the physical intimacy generating that feeling, either. Sometimes he simply looked at her and it seemed he knew her through and through, as though they had lived a whole life together and there were no secrets between them. Which was ridiculous. And disturbing.

Only Zachary Lee had ever looked at her like that, understanding without need for any spoken words. But her big brother did have a knowledge of her that Adam Cazell didn't. Or was Adam gifted with amazing intuition? Certainly as a lover he was sensitive to every nuance of her response to him.

She moved her gaze from the spectacle of the party revels, fastening it on the profile of the man who had made her feel so much pleasure in being a woman. Pleasure in simply being with him, too. She liked him—liked looking at him, talking to him, even touching him, feeling his very male strength. Rebel had been right. She was safe with him. But she wasn't safe from the emotions he stirred.

'You don't *have* to leave, do you, Rosalie?' he said quietly, breaking the comfortable silence between them. 'You're choosing to go.' He turned his head, his eyes scouring hers for the reason. 'Would you mind telling me why?'

'I stayed longer than I meant to, Adam,' she excused, not really capable of explaining the confused sense of losing some critical part of whom she'd been before coming here.

'I know.' His mouth curled into a wry smile. 'You came to have a need fulfilled and a question answered. That only took one night.'

Again she felt a squirming wave of shame at her initial intention to use him for her own satisfaction. 'I thought you'd be getting what you wanted, too.'

'An itch soothed?' he mocked, his eyes deriding this shallow view of him.

'You didn't really know me as a person,' she argued.

'I knew that I wanted to know you. Mind, heart and soul, Rosalie. Not just your body.' His gaze drifted down to travel over the feminine curves he now knew so intimately. 'Which is very beautiful,' he added softly, then lifted his gaze to hers again. 'But I've known others who were also beautiful in their own way. That was not the experience I sought from you. I think we have much more to give each other.'

She felt a rush of panic at the claim he was making on her mind and heart and soul. It was one thing to trust him with her body, quite another to entwine herself so deeply with him that her ability to act on her own was compromised because she'd be missing him all the time.

'Adam, this has been a kind of idyllic time. And I thank you for it.'

'But you want it contained here.'

'Yes,' she said, immensely relieved that he understood.

'Because you think it will be different once we're back in the world?'

'It can't be the same. There'll be other demands on us. You know that, Adam.'

'Our time together would obviously be considerably limited, but to me that would make it even more special.'

'And what if I'm not around when you want me around?' She raised a deliberately challenging eyebrow. 'You're a man who's used to getting what you want, Adam. How soon before you step in and interfere with my life because you're frustrated with the situation?'

He shook his head. 'I'm well aware that I'd always come second to your work, Rosalie, and if I tried to come first I'd lose you. I thought we could both make some reasonable accommodations.'

'Can't you see I don't fit?' she flashed at him from the inner angst he was stirring. 'I'm not a party person. I'd only want...'

She stopped, appalled that she had almost admitted the still churning desire to prolong this relationship beyond what was sensible or even practical, given her commitment to other things. More important things, she fiercely told herself. Adam didn't need saving but countless children did.

'You'd only want what we've had here,' he finished for her.

'It's not possible,' she stated emphatically, wishing she hadn't conceded anything.

'The place doesn't matter, Rosalie. It's how we

spend the time together. And I assure you I wouldn't want to waste it on a social whirl with other people.'

'Please...stop!' Her eyes begged for relief from being pressed. 'I have a mission. You don't fit into it, Adam.'

His gaze burned with a steady intensity. 'I could. If you'd allow me to...'

'No! Whatever you did would only be for me and I don't want to feel beholden to you.'

'I give to a lot of charities. None of them feel beholden to me.'

'It's just money. You're not personally involved with them.'

'But money buys equipment that helps. I could supply whatever you thought was needed in your orphanages. You could tell me about it...'

'And then I'd be dependent on you,' she cried.

'Is that so terrible?'

'Let me go, Adam. Just let me go.'

It was a desperate, tortured plea. She wrenched her gaze from his and stared blindly out to sea, drawing her legs up on the rug and hugging them, subconsciously making herself smaller so she didn't feel so exposed to him and his attack on a decision that had to be right. All these years of commitment to rescuing children in need held more meaning to her than any one on one relationship.

He fell silent but the silence was no relief. It tore at nerves already stressed by having to fight his strong attraction. It raised tormenting doubts in her mind. She hated the idea of leaving him feeling *used* by her.

But she had given him something of herself. More than she'd given any other person. And it wasn't as though it hadn't been a mutual desire being pursued. And satisfied. There was no reason to feel this burden of guilt, as though she had denied him some further right to her.

'What about Cate, Rosalie?' he asked. 'She thinks you're her friend. Are you cutting her off, too?'

It sounded callous, brutal, but there was only so much of her to go around. 'I hope I've made some positive difference to her life, Adam. It's all I can do.'

'All you *choose* to do,' he sliced back at her with a sudden savagery that cut her to the quick.

The tension inside her erupted. Words flew from her mouth, exploding from the sealed compartments in her brain and powering through the emotional pressure he was laying on her.

'I didn't *choose* a father who didn't care to know me or look after me. I didn't *choose* a mother who was little more than a prostitute, whose death gave some of her lowlife companions the idea of using me for their dirty profit. I didn't *choose* to be kidnapped and locked up in a house where children were supplied to rich, foreign paedophiles...'

'Paedophiles!'

His shock fed some weird satisfaction inside her, driving her on. 'I didn't *choose* to witness what hap-

pened to some of those children, but there was no
escape from it, and I knew my turn was coming. The
evil men who ran that place talked about me as a prize
who'd fetch a very high price and they were keeping
me for one particular client...'

'You were only seven!'

'There were some there younger,' she hurled at
him. 'Some who died from their injuries. And if
Zachary Lee hadn't been an investigative journalist at
the time, hadn't broken that wicked ring wide open
and rescued me...'

The fierce torrent of words died in a shuddering
sigh. She clamped her mouth shut and closed her
eyes, wanting to block out the memories that had
burst from her with so much explosive force. She'd
never told anyone this. Of course, the James family
knew. They all knew about each other. But no one
else. Never anyone else. And why she'd told Adam
now...she shook her head. Some deep clawing need
for him to understand? To let her go...

'There are other children out there...in similar circumstances,' she choked out over the huge lump
forming in her throat.

'It's okay, Rosalie,' he said gently. 'I see where
you're coming from. I see where you have to go.'

'Cate has you.'

'Yes. She has me.' He heaved a deep sigh and murmured, 'And who am I to clip an angel's wings?'

The silence was not so stressful this time though it
held a weight of sadness that Rosalie sensed was

shared by both of them. They sat apart, and she felt
his loneliness as much as she felt her own. It hurt.
They had been so close the last few days. But there
was a bigger picture than just the two of them and a
greater hurt that needed to be prevented...at all costs.
How could she think of limiting her aid and taking
what this man offered?

Would he be a helpmate to her?

Could she trust him not to interfere, not to pressure
her into doing less and less?

Wouldn't the heart-tearing anguish she felt now
just be repeated again and again and again if she tried
to continue a relationship with him?

Better that it be stopped now. The decision was
made. Adam had accepted it. Tomorrow she would
leave and get on with her own life.

Adam slowly and painfully came to the conclusion
there was nothing he could do or say to alter Rosalie's
decision. Her life was built from her experience as a
child and her memories—his jaw clenched as he en-
visaged the images that were stamped so traumati-
cally on her mind—could never be erased or even
diminished. She would live with them forever.

He felt incredibly privileged that she had chosen
him—of all the men she could have had—to show
her that sex could be an act of loving, not hurting,
that it could be about giving pleasure, not taking it
with brutal disregard for the other person. He
hoped...no, he knew she had that understanding now,

and at least it would have contributed some measure of good to balance against the bad.

But letting her go…

Just the thought of losing her was gut-wrenching. Everything within him wanted to fight to keep her, if only partially in his life. He could and would help her in her mission, but getting her to accept that…now wasn't the time. With the realisation of what he was dealing with—no mystery anymore—he knew he had to give her the space she was demanding, the freedom to act according to her conscience.

Maybe it was his own need arguing that the connection between them was too strong for a clean cut to be possible. Maybe Rosalie could put him and everything they'd shared behind her. He just couldn't bring himself to believe it. Destiny had a strange way of working. He was convinced they had been meant to meet, that he was the one man for her, she the woman for him, and they *would* meet again because this was not enough. Not for either of them.

There was still some time left here. With a sense of intense urgency, Adam searched his mind for how best to break this silence and reach out to her again, bring her back to him for this one last night on Tortola. The way she was sitting—her body language alone told him she was in deep retreat, probably from the shock of having opened up to him, spilling out what was terribly private and personal.

Had she ever confided her background to anyone else?

No. Adam felt an absolute certainty on that point. It would only be the strength of their connection that had released those secrets and she hadn't connected like this with anyone else. He had to regain and reinforce the bond she had felt with him.

'Thank you for telling me, Rosalie,' he said quietly.

She sat like a stone statue, staring blindly out to sea.

'You have my solemn promise that no one else will ever get knowledge of that part of your life from me. It's safe.'

She sighed and moved her head slightly to flash him a sadly ironic smile. 'Safe,' she repeated, her dark eyes filled with a darkness he couldn't read. He sensed pain. 'I didn't even think of…of possible gossip.'

'You don't have to. It won't happen.'

'I guess…I guess…I have to trust you.'

'You can. And you have trusted me, Rosalie, with far more than what you were driven to speak. The gift of yourself was…is…something I will always value very deeply. And that, too, is an absolutely private thing, belonging only to us.'

Her eyes shone with the welling moistness of tears. 'Thank you, Adam,' she said huskily.

'Take my hand.'

He held it out to her and after a moment's hesitation she unfolded her arms, reached out and surrendered her hand to his, letting him reforge the physical link between them. It felt fragile, uncertain, yet there was trust implicit in it, belief that he meant her no harm and would do whatever was in his power to ensure none came to her through him.

'After you're gone tomorrow, I'll explain to Cate that your involvement with both of us was a gift of caring about our relationship and how it should be. I'll put it in perspective for her so she'll understand it wasn't intended to be...something lasting.'

Though it was, Adam thought, and felt Rosalie's fingers tighten around his, an instinctive, anguished protest against separation, revealing the torn nature of past needs and current desires.

'I'd...I'd appreciate that. Tell her I'm sorry...if I raised expectations...I can't fulfil.'

He nodded, running his thumb over the underside of her wrist, feeling the agitated leap of her pulse. 'So let's set this aside now, Rosalie, and make our last evening here a happy one together. Okay?'

A tautly held breath whooshed out. Her shoulders slumped in relief. She flashed him a grateful smile. 'That would be good.'

Rosalie hoped she gave no sign of any underlying stress while the party on the beach raged on. Cate ducked back and forth from the dancing, picking up cans of diet Coke and regaling them with the wild and funny antics she'd seen or engaged in, her high spirits infectious enough to make Rosalie laugh at her reports.

Between his daughter's haphazard visits for liquid

refreshment, Adam did his best to entertain her with his own amusing commentary on island activities. He recounted the odd English influences that the native population had adopted as right and proper, the anomalies like driving on the left of the road in American vehicles designed to be driven on the right, the bandaged people who were occasionally seen shopping in Road Town, clients of a very secluded clinic on the island where very discreet facelifts were done.

It passed the time easily enough until Cate was ready to go home. The trip back to the villa seemed all too short. The *family* part of the night was over with Cate declaring she was totally laid waste and heading straight for bed. Which left Rosalie alone with Adam, acutely conscious of how she had spent every other night here with him, desperately wanting the intimacy they'd shared yet feeling hopelessly awkward about it, having virtually ended any hope of a continuance.

Adam was holding her hand again but it was more a friendly link, not a sexual one. Maybe she had killed his desire for her, telling him about the horror of her childhood. Or maybe he felt she had already removed herself from any deeper physical closeness with him. She started wriggling her fingers free of his hold, wanting to bolt to her bedroom because she simply couldn't face more talk.

He turned to her, recapturing her hand, grasping the other and lifting them both to rest palms open on his chest, holding them there, forcing her to feel the heat of his body and the pounding of his heart.

'Rosalie…'

She shot a pained gaze up to his and her own heart instantly kicked into a thunderous beat. There was no mistaking the naked wanting in his eyes, the intensity of the appeal he put into words.

'Will you be with me…give me…tonight? All night?'

She had left him to go to her own suite every other night, wary of giving him the idea she was committed to an ongoing affair, needing to keep some integral part of herself to herself, away from the enthralment of how he made her feel with him. But he knew it was the end now. They both did. There was nothing dishonest or misleading about staying with him. And she wanted one last beautiful memory to take with her.

'Yes. Yes, I will, Adam,' she promised him in a soft, yearning whisper.

He enfolded her in his arms and the warm comfort of his embrace soothed the ache inside her. Her hands slid up around his neck and buried themselves in his thick, wavy hair, revelling in touching him again. Their lips met in a kiss that melted any sense of loneliness, that breathed new life into the magic of being with this man.

Then with his arm curled around her shoulders, hugging her to his side, they walked to his suite where they undressed each other in a slow, silent ceremony, savouring every sensual pleasure given and taken.

'This isn't sex, Rosalie,' Adam murmured as he took her in his arms again and pressed soft, tender kisses to her temples, her eyelids, her nose. 'It's making love.'

And she understood that truth as his mouth claimed hers and her body instinctively strained to get as close to his as possible, because she didn't just *like* Adam Cazell. She *loved* all that he was and she wanted him to feel it, to let him know he wasn't just *an experience* to her. It was the one parting gift she could give and she gave it unreservedly, transmitting it in every touch, every response, her whole body attuned to loving…mind, heart and soul.

And when he was deep inside her, paused there for them both to revel in the sense of absolute union, she looked at him, her eyes filled with all the blissful emotion he stirred, and whispered, 'You'll always be part of me, Adam.'

'And you, me,' he answered.

It was a truth she took with her when she flew away from Tortola the next morning. It was a truth that haunted her in the days, weeks, months that followed. Regardless of how busy she made herself, regardless of her mission to save children who needed saving…

Adam Cazell could not be forgotten.

CHAPTER ELEVEN

ROSALIE had just returned to the Mayfair apartment and was sorting through the games she'd bought when the telephone rang. They were all games she'd played with Cate and Adam on Tortola and she'd been particularly impressed with the Rummikub one—a form of gin rummy played with tiles. She was planning another trip to Cambodia and thought the children in the orphanage would really enjoy something novel to play with.

'Hi! Rosalie James,' she announced into the receiver, not even wondering who the caller was, her mind lingering on memories of balmy afternoons on the villa verandah and the kind of *family* fun she'd shared over board games, Cate fiercely competitive with her father, but sweetly helpful to Rosalie who wasn't familiar with the rules.

'It's Rebel. I haven't seen you for ages and ages.'

Not since the day she'd met Adam Cazell at Davenport Hall.

'I've hardly been here,' Rosalie quickly excused.

'Come down to lunch tomorrow. It's the last day of Celeste's half-term break and she'd love to see you, too.'

Celeste was Cate's best friend. Was this a ruse to

set up a meeting? Rosalie sharply recalled her sister's persuasive part in pressing an involvement with the Cazells.

'Did Celeste bring anyone home with her?' she asked cautiously.

'No. It's just family. And I won't inflict other visitors on you,' she dryly added, well aware of Rosalie's anti-social attitude. 'Okay?'

The swift rise of tension abated. 'Okay. It will be good to see the boys, too.'

'I'll send the Rolls for you. Nine o'clock?'

'Fine.'

A family day… Rosalie gave herself a stern mental shake as she put the receiver down. She had always enjoyed being at Davenport Hall and it was stupid to avoid going there just because it would inevitably be a reminder of what she had turned away from. There was a plethora of reminders anyway, even the games she'd bought.

And in several telephone calls since her visit to Tortola, Rebel had only once mentioned Adam Cazell, rather tentatively asking if he had made a nuisance of himself since she'd given him the Mayfair number. Rosalie had assured her sister he'd been very much the gentleman, not pestering her at all, and she apologised for having been testy about Rebel's judgment of him. He had, indeed, been *safe*.

There'd been no gossip linking them together. Adam had made no attempt whatsoever to change the decision she'd made. There'd been no deliberate con-

tact, nor any *accidental* meeting. The only thing he'd
done was to press a business card on her before they
parted, insisting that she keep it in case she ever
wanted to call him for any reason whatsoever.

However, it did cross her mind now that Cate might
have told Celeste about her visit to Tortola, and if
Rebel was nursing that information…was the invitation to lunch an opportunity to probe?

Rosalie felt her nerves tightening up again and
heaved a deep sigh to relax them. So what if the subject of Adam did come up? She could deflect it
quickly enough and her sister wouldn't tread too
heavily on sensitive ground.

As it turned out, neither Celeste nor Rebel mentioned the Cazells. Rosalie was warmly welcomed at
Davenport Hall. They were all delighted to see her.
Geoffrey and Malcolm instantly demanded she play
with them, and after a very congenial morning tea,
they carted her off to their playroom where Daddy
had set out a wonderful Grand Prix race track. She
was given a remote control to race the blue car against
the red car and the green car. Geoffrey had to show
her not to go too fast around the corners so the car
would not zip off the track.

Over lunch, Celeste peppered her with questions
over fashion matters, particularly the pret-a-porter
shows in Paris, explaining that the girls at school
would want to know what Rosalie thought would be
the most popular new trends for the coming winter.

Reminded strongly of Cate's obsession about being

thin, Rosalie hoped Adam's daughter was following a better balanced eating plan now. She noticed Celeste did not hesitate to eat a slice of strawberry cheesecake for dessert, but her adopted niece had a very sensible mother in Rebel, one who would instantly crack down on unhealthy fads where her children were concerned.

The question slipped out before Rosalie realised what she was saying. 'How is your friend, Cate Cazell?'

'Cate? She's great! Scored the winning goal in our last hockey match,' Celeste answered with glee.

'Well, good for her!' The relief of not having opened up a potentially personal landmine encouraged her to satisfy the need to know more. 'I thought she was...unhappy within herself...when she was here at the beginning of the summer vacation,' she remarked, her eyes questioning.

Celeste shrugged. 'Cate had a thing about her parents not really caring about her. That seems to be all sorted out now.'

'I'm glad to hear it.' Somehow she couldn't stop herself from asking, 'Is she with her father for this school break?'

'No. He's in Hong Kong. But she had a whole lot of stuff planned with her mother so she was happy about being with her in London.'

'That's good.'

Celeste turned to Hugh, asking what time he wanted to drive her back to Roedean and Rosalie silently and painfully reflected that it had been stupid to feel a sense of belonging with the Cazells. Adam was half a world away, going about his business as usual. Cate had a mother who was obviously giving more attention to satisfying her daughter's needs. The part Rosalie had played in their lives was done.

And why that should make her feel depressed she didn't know. She had chosen to be alone. It was easier to do what she did independently of others. No strings attached. Nothing owed to anyone.

She should be pleased that she had accomplished some good, at least for Cate. Adam had certainly shown himself to be a more caring and observant father on the island, and...what was his ex-wife's name? Married to the British MP, Gerald Mayberry. Sarah...yes, that was it. Sarah had apparently been enlightened on her parental responsibility by Adam.

So there was nothing to feel down about.

Nevertheless, when Rebel asked her to stay on and keep her company while Hugh returned Celeste to school, Rosalie was quick to oblige, relieved to put off going home to a lonely apartment. Her sister was always bright and cheerful, and any conversation was better than silence right now.

Though when she was roped into bathing the boys, ready for bed, she found her mind roving back to what Adam had said about having a child of her own. Geoffrey and Malcolm were such darlings and Rebel adored them. When Rosalie had queried her about having brought *more* children into the world, her sister had declared she was bringing up her boys to have a social conscience, and the world certainly needed more people who had that.

'What happens when you die, Rosalie?' had come the challenging counter. 'Who will carry on your work? We've been so lucky to be part of the James family. Don't you think what was done for us should never be lost?'

Continuance…

It was important.

There just hadn't been a man who'd ever given Rosalie pause to consider marriage and family for herself. And there was no point in linking Adam to that idea now. Too late….

Once the boys were put to bed, Rebel linked arms with her as they strolled downstairs again. Her eyes twinkled triumphant pleasure as she said, 'You see? Whatever you said to Adam Cazell about Cate did make a difference. She's not at risk anymore.'

'I hope not.'

'What about you, Rosalie? Still happy to whizz around the world, doing good where you can?'

'It's rewarding.'

Her sister sighed. 'Well, I do think you should have given Adam Cazell a chance. I liked him.'

'Mmmh…'

'Okay, okay, I promised not to push anyone at you and I won't. Let's go to the TV room and watch the news while we're waiting for Hugh. He shouldn't be too late for dinner.'

They settled in armchairs, Rebel having poured them both small glasses of sherry as pre-dinner drinks. The television provided a focus that precluded any need to make conversation. Rosalie rarely drank much alcohol but she was contemplating drowning out her thoughts tonight. No worries about drink-driving. Hugh's chauffeur would see her safely home when it was time to go and she could fall asleep in the Rolls.

The news commentary was a meaningless blur until Rebel gasped, 'Oh, my God!'

The screen was showing the wreckage of an expensive car. 'What?' Rosalie queried.

'Listen!' came the urgent command.

'...member of parliament, and his wife, Sarah, were rushed to hospital but both were declared dead on arrival. Mrs Mayberry's daughter was returned to her school earlier this evening and is waiting for her father, well-known British billionaire, Adam Cazell, to return from Hong Kong...'

'Cate!' Rosalie leapt to her feet, the sherry spilling over the glass in her agitation. 'She must know her mother's dead and she has no one with her.'

'The headmistress would have taken her under her wing. I hope she's not seeing this. Look at the car...' Rebel was shaking her head in appalled horror.

Rosalie spun on her, shouting to break through the shock. 'She's just lost her mother. *Her mother,* Rebel! Remember how that feels? Do you think a headmistress can give her what she needs? And it's almost a fourteen hour flight from Hong Kong. It will be to-morrow morning before Adam can get to her.'

Rebel looked bewildered. 'But what can we do? We're not relatives, Rosalie.'

'We're friends. We're sympathetic friends. She likes it here. We can go and get her. Cate has to be with people who care. Who'll look after her...'

Rebel was on her feet. She whipped the glass from Rosalie's wildly gesticulating hand, set it down, then grabbed her upper arms. 'Listen up! We have no right...'

'Adam will give me the right.' She tore herself out of Rebel's grasp and driven by unshakable purpose, headed for the sitting room where she'd left her hand-bag. 'I'll call him. Call him now.'

Her sister followed, crying out what she obviously thought was sensible logic. 'How on earth do you think you can contact him in Hong Kong? Or in flight if he's already on his way home?'

'Adam gave me a number and said I could reach him on it anywhere, anytime, for any reason.' She was already hunting through her wallet for his card. 'Cate shouldn't be left on her own tonight.'

'Rosalie...you barely know the man.'

'I know him.' She flashed a hard, impatient look at her sister. 'You said I should give him a chance and I did. It was good. I spent days with him and Cate on a Caribbean island...'

Rebel's mouth dropped open in shock.

'...and I can't stand back and do nothing when Adam isn't here for her.'

'Right!' The dropped jaw clicked back into place though her eyes still looked dazed. 'Call him then. I'm with you.'

Rosalie whipped out the card and carried it to the great entrance hall where the closest telephone was situated. She dialled the number, determined purpose thumping through her heart, not even pausing to consider she was re-forging a connection with the Cazells, remembering only too vividly how frightened and lost and empty she'd felt when told her mother was dead. No one had taken her hand or hugged her to make her feel safe. She'd been left alone...

'Adam Cazell...'

His voice was curt, tense, the pent-up need for fast action coursing through it, just as it was coursing through her.

'It's Rosalie, Adam.'

'Rosalie...' The pained yearning in his voice struck deep chords, reawakening the hurt of parting, the ache of not being with him.

'I'm at Davenport Hall,' she said quickly. 'I want to go and get Cate and bring her here, be with her until you come. She may need me, Adam.'

'Yes.' Intense relief. 'I spoke to her earlier. She's totally distraught, Rosalie.' A deeply scooped in breath, then gruffly, 'Thank you for thinking of her.'

Her stomach contracted. She was thinking of him, too, wanting the togetherness they'd known, needing contact, being part of him. Even so, she fiercely concentrated her mind on what had to be done. 'Will you call the headmistress, clear the way?'

'At once.'

'Are you still in Hong Kong?'

'No. I left as soon as word reached me. I'm in flight to London.'

'Come here when you land. It will be more private for both of you.'

He was a very public figure. Cate's stepfather had also been one. There'd be reporters. She didn't care for herself. Comforting Cate and protecting her from the media was far more important.

'Yes.' No need to spell it out to Adam. He knew. His voice was furred with intense gratitude. 'Thank you. And thank Rebel and Hugh for me.'

'I will.'

'Rosalie…' Just the way he said her name tugged on her heart so strongly, a lump of emotion welled up her throat. 'It's a big help…knowing you'll be with Catie.'

The emotion conveyed in calling his daughter Catie rather than Cate brought tears to her eyes. She struggled to speak, heard Adam taking another deep breath and tried it herself.

'I'll call her,' he said more firmly. 'Tell her you're coming. It will mean a lot to her.'

She knew it meant a lot to him, as well, knew the line she'd drawn on Tortola had been crossed and there'd be no going back to separate lives. But she couldn't think about that now. This was a time for fast and effective action. And compassion. She swallowed hard, clearing her throat to speak.

'I'll set off now.' She swallowed again but her last heartfelt words were a bare whisper. 'Take care, Adam.'

Tears blurred her eyes as she set the receiver down. She turned blindly to Rebel who'd stood by transfixed, listening to the one-sided conversation with Adam. 'Will you call your chauffeur...to bring the Rolls around?' Rosalie choked out.

Rebel snapped into purposeful action. 'Of course. And I'll call Hugh on his car 'phone. He can backtrack, be there to lead you straight to Cate when we arrive. Being the Earl of Stanthorpe can be very handy to cut through fuss and give us a smooth passage. Oh, and tell Mrs. Tomkins and Brooks what we're about. They can watch over the boys. And a room needs to be prepared for Cate. For Adam, too, if he wants to stay.'

She pounced on the telephone and Rosalie rushed off to carry out her instructions, grateful that her sister now had her mind set on practicalities. The housekeeper and butler of Davenport Hall were quick to take in the emergency and respond to it. Within ten minutes she and Rebel were in the back seat of the Rolls-Royce and on their way to Roedean.

The first half hour of the trip to Sussex was travelled in silence. Rosalie appreciated the uninterrupted time to recollect her composure and focus her thoughts on how Cate would be feeling, having spent these past few days with her mother, saying goodbye to her without any warning it would be a final good-bye.

Rebel stirred, turning a sympathetic face to her. 'Do you want to talk about your relationship with the Cazells, Rosalie?' she asked softly.

'No.' It was too personal, too intimate, too private, and she didn't know where it was going. She grimaced an apology for the bluntly negative reply. 'It will work itself out...one way or another, Rebel.'

A nod of acknowledgment, then silence again.

Rosalie was remembering the words she'd spoken to Adam on their last night together—*You'll always be a part of me*—and his reply—*And you, me.*

Half a world might be separating them but the physical distance was irrelevant. The passage of time since Tortola meant nothing, either. When she'd been speaking to him on the 'phone, it had felt exactly the same—minds, hearts, souls touching in a unison that went beyond any rational understanding. There'd been no need to explain anything. And in that tacit acceptance of what they shared lay some future path.

But that had to wait.

Reaching Cate came first.

CHAPTER TWELVE

ROSALIE had no hesitation in walking into the headmistress's sitting room where Cate was waiting for her. She'd been warned that Adam's daughter was in deep shock. The girl had not spoken except to her father. Food offered had not been eaten. No tears had been shed.

This had been reported to Mr. Cazell when he'd called to direct that custody of his daughter be given to Rosalie James. He had not wanted Cate to be disturbed or treated by a doctor. She was to go with Ms. James who would look after her for him at the Earl of Stanthorpe's residence.

So much trust was riding on her shoulders but Rosalie didn't flinch from it. She closed the door quietly behind her, knowing Rebel would now be organising their departure from Roedean, having a word to Celeste, packing Cate's clothes, taking her bag down. Her sister would ride with Hugh in his car, Rosalie and Cate to ride together in the Rolls. Her only task was to reach past the block Cate was subconsciously using to shut out what was unbearable.

She was sitting by a window, staring blindly out into the night. Darkness was better than light to a traumatised mind. It hid what couldn't be looked at.

Rosalie knew this from her work with rescued children who were too frightened to accept that they *were* rescued.

But she believed trust had been established between herself and Cate, and the rapport they'd shared in the past would no more have been lost than it had been between her and Adam. As she crossed the room she picked up a chair and placed it at right angles to Cate's so it wasn't directly confrontational, but close enough to reach out to her. The girl did not acknowledge her, not by glance or word, even when she sat down next to her.

'Cate, it's Rosalie,' she announced quietly. 'I'm sorry about your mother. I know you were with her these past few days, and I hope they were good days for you.'

The girl's jaw tightened. Her throat moved in a convulsive swallow.

'I hope it was the best time ever,' Rosalie gently pressed.

Cate's head jerked around, her eyes filled with pain. 'She's dead. I'll never see her again.'

'I know.' She reached out and took one of the suddenly clenched fists from the girl's lap, stroking to ease the fighting tension. 'I know you'll only have memories of your mother now, and they'll never fill what you need from her, but you do know that she loved you and wanted to give you the best of everything. That's a memory you must keep alive because it's very precious and it's the one expression of your love for her that you can put into practice by striving to be the best person you can be—a daughter she'd be proud to have given birth to.'

Tears welled into her eyes. 'I didn't say it, Rosalie. I didn't say I loved her.'

'Your smile, your laughter, the happiness in your eyes, your kiss goodbye...all those things told your mother that you loved her. She knew, Cate. Believe me. She didn't need the words to tell her so.'

'She listened to me this time. She really did. But I didn't tell her how much it meant to...to...' Her voice choked on a sob.

'To feel you were a real part of her life?' Rosalie finished sympathetically, then shook her head. 'It would have meant a lot to her, too, being a real part of yours. Sometimes we busy ourselves with so many outside interests, the one special bond we should value most gets pushed aside. But it's not lost. It's too strong a bond to be lost. And when it comes first, it's wonderful for both of you, Cate. That doesn't have to be said. It just is.'

Tears were rolling down her cheeks but she looked directly at Rosalie and asked, 'Do you feel a bond with me and Daddy?'

The answer welled straight from her heart. 'Yes. And I'm here for you, Cate. To hold you safe for your father while he's flying back to you.' She took her other hand and pressed gently. 'Will you come to Davenport Hall with me?'

She nodded.

Rosalie stood and drew Cate to her feet. The girl wobbled slightly and Rosalie dropped her hands and drew her into a tight hug, feeling the slight body sag against hers and arms flying around her waist to hold on. She softly stroked her hair and back, imparting all the comfort she could as Cate wept on her shoulder.

Eventually the heaving sobs eased into shuddering little sighs. 'Does Daddy know I'll be at Davenport Hall?' came the woebegone question.

'Yes. He'll come straight there from the airport, Cate.'

Another deep sigh, then, 'I'm okay to go now, Rosalie.'

There was no delay in their departure from the school. Hugh and the headmistress saw them into the Rolls. Rebel was standing by Hugh's Jaguar, waiting to take off ahead of them. She gave the thumbs up sign, a silent assurance that everything would be ready when they arrived.

Once they were on their way, Rosalie encouraged Cate to recount the whole half-term break with her mother, knowing that talking would be the best release for pent-up feelings and she'd be able to ease any lingering sense of guilt that inevitably came with the thought of *if only…*

The sudden bereavement was bad enough. The sense of being cheated of all the years ahead was hard to come to terms with. But there really was no cause for guilt to weave its insidious way through Cate's emotions and Rosalie kept focusing on the positive things that had happened during the half-term break, trying to make Cate feel glad that she'd had the chance to get close to her mother again.

By the time they arrived at Davenport Hall Rosalie knew that exhaustion had set in. Rebel led them up to the bedroom suite that had been prepared for Cate, who was too worn out to even attempt to eat anything. A mug of hot chocolate was all she could manage. Rosalie tucked her into bed and sat by her, holding her hand. They still talked, but only in a piecemeal fashion...random thoughts, comforting assurances. Eventually Cate went to sleep.

Rebel had moved a big winged armchair and footstool close to the bed, along with cushions and a rug so that Rosalie could make herself comfortable. A nearby traymobile held flasks of soup and hot chocolate, as well as a supply of buttered bread rolls and freshly cooked muffins. Rosalie looked at it all but she had no appetite for anything. She settled herself in the armchair, intent on keeping watch over Cate for the night.

Adam would come in the morning.

She didn't let herself think beyond that.

It was for Cate, Adam kept telling himself. He must not read anything more into Rosalie's act of compassion. Somehow she'd heard he was in Hong Kong and she'd thought instantly of his daughter being alone and in need.

God knew how many traumatised children she'd helped over the years. He was deeply grateful that she'd been here to give Cate her hand and heart through this horror of Sarah's death. To press her for what *he* wanted...wrong time, wrong place, wrong everything. It couldn't be done.

Yet it had been months—long empty months—since Tortola and this was his first chance to...no, it couldn't be done!

Adam had this fixed firmly in his mind when he finally arrived at Davenport Hall. One of his company limousines was being chauffered for his convenience and as soon as it was brought to a halt, he was out, having instructed the driver to wait until further notice.

Even as he hurried up the steps one of the great entrance doors to the hall was opened by the butler. The elderly man gave him a grave nod. 'Good morning, sir.'

'Good morning,' Adam automatically returned. It was only seven-thirty but obviously someone had been posted to watch for his arrival so he could be fast-forwarded to his daughter. It cemented his impression of the Davenports as kind, generous people.

Rebel was standing just inside the great entrance hall. 'Adam,' she greeted quickly. 'You made good time.'

'The advantage of owning an airline.'

'Brooks, please take care of Mr. Cazell's chauffeur.'

'Certainly, m'lady.'

She hooked her arm around Adam's and led him down the hall to the grand staircase at the end of it as she delivered information. 'Cate is still asleep. Rosalie has sat beside her all night in case she needed soothing but the sleep has been deep and peaceful. The two of them talked for a long time so I think the talking eased Cate's mind.' She flashed him a sympathetic look. 'I am sorry about her mother, Adam. Such a dreadful end to a life.'

'The worst possible time,' he returned with a grimace. 'I'd spoken to Sarah about Cate's need for more of her attention and from what Cate told me, her mother was giving it. Which makes the loss even more acute. I deeply appreciate your having her here. Very good of you.'

'Hugh and I were only too pleased to have the opportunity to help. Rosalie...' She paused, looked at him with eyes that both searched and appealed. '...she's a very special person, Adam.'

Was it a warning?

'I know,' he said quietly. 'The most special person I've ever known.'

The assurance of his feeling for her sister seemed to both satisfy and vex. 'No meddling,' she muttered under her breath as they started up the stairs.

Of course she had to be curious about their association, Adam thought. He wondered how much Rosalie had told her to explain involving herself with his daughter. Minimal information, he decided. What they'd shared would be kept very private, but there was no denying a bond between them. Which gave him some hope for the future.

'There's an in-house communication system on the bedside table in Cate's room,' Rebel went on matter-of-factly. 'Please call for any service you'd like. Do you need some refreshment brought up to you now? Coffee, tea…?'

'No. I'll wait until Cate wakes. Thank you, Rebel.'

'You and Cate are welcome to stay at Davenport Hall as long as you like. Please don't feel you have to hurry off.'

'Thank you again for your kind hospitality, but we'll go when Cate is ready. I think she'll want to be home with me in London.'

'Yes. When it comes right down to it, there's no running away from what has to be faced,' she sadly remarked. 'It's feeling loved and cared for that helps turn the corner.'

It made him wonder what Rebel—another child adopted into the James family—had come from? Which brought him back to Rosalie's mission. No doubt her sister supported it, yet he sensed she supported his cause in pursuing a relationship with Rosalie, too. Perhaps an ally, if one was of any use.

They reached the corridor on the first upper floor. Rebel steered him to the left and they walked almost to the end of a long wing, halting at a door which had been left slightly ajar so there'd be no noise with opening or closing. 'They're in here. I'll leave you to it, Adam,' Rebel murmured, withdrawing her arm and turning back the way they'd come.

Adam braced himself for a meeting he had been convinced would happen, but not in these circumstances. Every muscle in his body was gripped with tension as he forced the necessary discipline into his mind. Rosalie was here for Cate, he recited, but his heart was thundering in his chest, not in tune with that dictate, beating a savage belief that she was here for him, too. He tried to ignore it, pushing himself into action, his hand reaching out to open the door wide enough for him to enter.

The room was dark, curtains drawn, but the opening door let in enough light for him to see this wasn't merely a bedroom, but a very large guest suite; armchairs grouped on either side of a fireplace, a writing-desk set in front of a window, table and chairs, a bookcase, television set...

He took a deep breath and stepped inside. A huge four-poster bed hit his gaze—Cate's head, motionless on the pillows. And there was Rosalie, rising from an armchair beside the bed, her face very pale, tired, but her dark velvet eyes locking onto his, beaming a silent, forceful message not to move or speak.

He didn't even breathe as he watched her come to him, unable to stop himself from feasting on every detail of her...the spill of her silky black hair over her shoulders, the dark plum coloured sweater that hugged the curves of her breasts and accentuated her small waist, the black slacks that encased her long, beautiful legs. She gestured for him to step back into the corridor and he just managed to recollect himself enough to do so and focus his mind on Cate again.

'How is she?' he asked as soon as Rosalie had pulled the door almost closed behind them.

'Better for talking through her thoughts and feelings with me, Adam, but please understand she'll cling to you today, and you must give her a strong sense of security with you. Don't go out anywhere and leave her, not for anything. She'll be afraid of losing you, too. It's not a fear you can reason with and it won't go away quickly.'

Her advice made instant sense to him. 'Understood,' he said, responding to the urgent intensity in her voice, her eyes. 'Thank you for all you've done, Rosalie.'

A ghost of a smile as the urgency faded. 'Thank you for trusting me.'

He'd trust her with his life. And Cate's.

Maybe she sensed the fierce wave of emotion flooding through him, or saw it in his eyes. She stepped away from him, nodding to the door, 'You'd better go in now, Adam.'

Instinctively his hand reached out to her. 'Don't go before we leave.' The words burst from his need to say much more.

'I won't,' she softly assured him. 'I'll be in the sitting room.'

Huge relief. 'Thank you.'

She nodded again and turned to go.

He didn't want to watch her walking away from him.

He stepped back into the room where Cate would see him the moment she awoke.

CHAPTER THIRTEEN

CATE leaned forward from the back seat of the limousine, looking past Adam to Rosalie who'd stood back for the chauffeur to shut their door. 'Tomorrow...you promise?' she checked anxiously.

'I promise,' came the firm assurance.

Adam's frustration was considerably eased by that promise as the limousine moved slowly around the large stone fountain and headed down the avenue that took them away from Davenport Hall. It didn't matter that she was only coming for a simple afternoon tea, pressed into it by Cate's plea for help on what to wear for her mother's funeral. It was another chance to be with her, a chance to talk of other things.

She had refused his invitation to dine with them tonight. 'As a thank you,' he had insisted. She'd shaken her head and answered, 'Not appropriate, Adam,' and her eyes had known what he really wanted.

Whether she wanted it, too, had been impossible to gauge. He'd been fighting to contain the rampant desire to just sweep her into his embrace and kiss her into submission. That, too, had been impossible...in front of Cate.

But tomorrow he'd make some time alone with her.

He would speak, regardless of the decision she'd made on Tortola, press for a change of mind, offer her everything at his disposal to give, anything as long as he could persuade her to take some place in his life.

'Remember what you said about Rosalie on Tortola, Dad? That we had to let her go because a lot of children in terrible circumstances depended on her?'

He winced at the reminder. 'Yes, I remember.'

There'd been no other choice then.

Maybe there still wasn't, but given half a chance he'd test her decision to the limits. They belonged together. And right now his body was in total rebellion against accepting another long separation.

He was sorry Sarah was dead. Especially sorry for Cate. Yet the base truth was, he'd moved past any love he'd felt for his ex-wife a long time ago. It was Rosalie who consumed the centre of his universe. Everything else was peripheral.

'Last night when Rosalie came for me...' Cate looked at him hopefully. 'She said she felt a bond with us, Dad.'

'Yes. That much is true.' He sighed and threw her a rueful little smile. 'But it doesn't mean she will stay with us, Cate. Don't count on it, sweetheart.'

This drew a frown. 'She makes me feel...I don't know. It just feels good with her.'

'It's how she makes me feel, too. And probably all

the children she helps. In Phnom Penh, they call her the angel.'

'The angel,' Cate repeated wistfully. She turned her head, staring out the side window, thinking her own thoughts.

Adam was fiercely thinking Rosalie was just as human as he was, enjoying the pleasure of their intimacy, revelling in it. She couldn't have forgotten how it was for them. He wouldn't let her forget.

After a while, Cate muttered, 'I guess angels know everything.' She turned pained eyes to him. 'She said Mummy did love me.'

'Of course she did.' He reached over and squeezed her hand. 'I love you, too.'

A big sigh. 'I wish…it could have always been like this half-term break with her. I was mean and cranky before…when she was too busy to bother with my things.'

'It's okay. Don't beat yourself up about it. Your mother understood that she'd been…neglecting you, Cate. She wanted to make it up to you.'

'Rosalie said…'

'Yes?'

She frowned, trying to get it right. 'It was about the special bond getting pushed aside because of other things. But it was never lost. It was always there…'

You'll always be a part of me.

'…and it was wonderful when it came first.'

Yes!

Hope soared through Adam's heart.

Tomorrow…

Afternoon tea… Rosalie's heart was in a helpless twist. Having given her word to Cate, she had to get through the couple of hours she'd be expected to stay, but seeing Adam again, feeling the sheer sexual magnetism of the man, the tug of his mind on hers…it just made the ache for him so much worse.

She could have been with him last night, could have shared the amazing intimacy that still haunted the dark hours before she went to sleep. And her dreams. His invitation had not been only for dinner. If she'd said yes, she might have said yes to much more, and then would come the temptation to fall into a part-time relationship with him, which would completely muddy the clear course she had mapped out for her life.

No more than a couple of hours, she determined as the limousine Adam had sent for her drew up outside his residence in Knightsbridge. It was a three storey building, facing a very pretty, enclosed park just across the street. Only a few blocks from Harrods, she thought, should Cate's clothes not be suitable for her mother's funeral. A quick shopping trip, afternoon tea in the food hall…it was a way out of being in Adam's company.

Unless he insisted on going with them.

And then she'd be alone with him while Cate tried on clothes.

The chauffeur opened the passenger door. With a

sigh of resignation, Rosalie braced herself to do her best for Cate while holding Adam's strong attraction at bay for the duration of this one unavoidable visit. She stepped out, crossed the sidewalk, and started mounting the steps to the front porch.

The front door was opened before she even reached it. Rosalie tensed, but it was not Adam facing her but Cate, obviously impatient for her arrival, wearing hipster jeans and a cropped sweater striped in dark blue and green, and looking relieved to see Rosalie.

'You're here!' came the unnecessary statement, conveying an uncertainty that was undoubtedly a reaction from having her mother ripped from her life.

Rosalie instantly focused her mind on giving the needed reassurance. She smiled. 'It wasn't far to come from Mayfair and riding in that huge limousine feels like riding in an armoured tank.'

It won a grin. 'It does kind of shut you away from the rest of the world, but it's a lot more cushy than a tank.'

'True. One is spoiled for comfort.'

Rosalie maintained the smile while stepping past Cate and pausing for her to close the door, but being inside Adam's home put her on edge, making it difficult to keep her facial muscles relaxed. Her mind was at war with the impulse to take everything in, know more about him, which would inevitably increase the colour and substance of memories that were already too vivid. She had to concentrate on Cate.

'Dad took me over to Mum's place this morning. I got the clothes she bought for me and a whole lot of other stuff I wanted to keep.' Her grimace told Rosalie it had been a stressful experience even before Cate added, 'I don't want to go back there.'

Too full of ghosts right now. 'You may want to later, Cate,' she said gently, hugging the girl's shoulders. 'Sometimes, it's good to revisit a place where a very memorable part of your life has happened, *after* you've moved on from it. You see it as…just a place…and you know the people you shared it with have moved on, too.'

'I guess…' she muttered, and heaved a deep sigh. 'I kept seeing Mum everywhere. I mean…not really seeing her but…'

'All her touches around the house.'

'Yeah…' Another sigh. 'Anyhow, I just shoved everything into bags so my room here is a bit of a mess at the moment.'

'Plenty of time to sort it out, Cate.'

'Mmmh…' She gestured to an opened door. 'Dad's in here.'

Rosalie surreptitiously took a deep breath as she entered the room, hoping to calm her nerves and give her brain a clearing shot of oxygen. Adam stood in front of a gas fire set in a black marble surround, above which was a spectacular Drysdale painting—a stark red-brown scene of the Australian Outback. Her peripheral vision picked up black leather sofas with geometrically patterned cushions in bright colours, but *he* completely dominated his surroundings.

A big man exuding power, not only from his impressive physique which was casually clothed in black jeans and a dark maroon shirt, but from his strongly boned, rugged-handsome face and the silver grey eyes that were so laser sharp with intelligence.

The intensity of his gaze instantly stripped Rosalie of any armour against the intimacy she had known with this man. The yearning to have it again flooded through her, an embarrassing heat that was mostly hidden by her black pantsuit and white blouse, but not even desperate willpower could diminish the warm tingle in her cheeks.

'It's good to have you here, Rosalie,' he said, making the statement feel very, very personal.

'Cate asked for my advice,' she returned, desperately trying to get herself back on an even keel.

He nodded. 'I'm glad she'll have the benefit of it.' He shifted his terribly unsettling gaze to his daughter. 'Cate, why don't you go up and try on what you think might be suitable out of the clothes you brought home, then come down and show both of us?'

'Okay,' she agreed.

Which spurred Rosalie into offering a safer option. 'Would you like me to come with you? Help select…'

'No, no…' She backed off, hands fluttering up in protest. 'You can hardly move in my room, it's such a mess. I'll do what Dad said.'

Leaving Rosalie alone with him.

The moment Cate was gone, Adam started towards her. She stood like a mesmerised dummy, her heart rocketing around her chest, feeling determined purpose engulfing her, seeing the glitter of reckless and uncontrollable desire in his eyes.

He plucked her handbag from her clutch, tossed it on the nearest sofa, took her hands, lifting them and pressing hot kisses onto their palms, then placing them on his shoulders, leaving them there as his arms encircled her, scooping her hard against him. His chest heaved under the soft press of her breasts. For a moment his head tilted back, chin jutting in an aggressive lift, then his gaze swept down, capturing hers in violent challenge.

'I've thought of holding you like this too many times. I need the reality of you, Rosalie. It's a need that claws at me night and day and won't let go because I know you're out there somewhere…and I want you.'

The passionate outburst, the strong hot imprint of his body on hers…both were direct and powerful hits on the need she felt for him. The mission that had driven her life was forgotten as his mouth crashed down on hers, and everything within her gloried in a wild sense of rightness as she welcomed him in to her inner self, kissing him back, revelling in the riotous sensations that claimed her mind and swirled through her body.

'You can't deny this! You can't!' he muttered fiercely as he broke the kiss to draw breath. His hand clamped around her head, pressed it onto his shoulder, his fingers clawing her hair as though desperate to reach into her brain. His lips were brushing her ear as he hoarsely whispered, 'We belong together. Say it! Admit it!'

She didn't want to say anything. She just wanted to savour the feel of him while she could. She closed her eyes and breathed in the scent of him, moved her face closer to his throat, tasted him.

'No!' She felt the word explode from him. He jerked away, stepped back, grabbing her upper arms, forcing her to look at him. 'I won't let you take what you want and leave me again. Understand this, Rosalie. You and I were made for each other. In far more than the sexual sense.'

Made for each other? The words bounced around her brain, not connecting to any overall certainty at all. Sexually, yes. The screaming need in her body attested to that truth…if there was such a truth *as being made for each other.* Her physical response to him was overwhelmingly positive. And the sense of belonging together was terribly strong. But there were other things…important things…that claimed her, too.

Her eyes begged mitigation from the accusation of *taking* him. 'I didn't start this, Adam.'

'Yes, you did, Rosalie. You called me.'

'Because you couldn't be there for Cate.'

'So you stood in for me. Because you and I are one.'

'No. Because…'

'Your mind and heart were instantly locked to mine and Cate's, Rosalie. A bond that no one else shares…has ever shared.'

'She needed someone who could help. That's what I do, Adam,' she pleaded.

'You called because you couldn't *not* call me. What flows between us is so strong…'

'I knew how she'd be,' Rosalie answered wildly, trying to fight off the assault of his willing her to accept more than she could let herself accept. Her memory supplied a host of children needing the same kind of help.

'And me. You knew how I'd be, too,' he threw back at her. 'Wanting you there for both of us.'

The passion in his voice made her temples throb. 'What are you asking of me?' she blurted out, her mind buckling under the pressure pouring from his.

'To let us into your life. Be part of it.'

'You are.'

'In spirit. But it can be much more than that, Rosalie. Partners, in every sense of the word.'

'You mean…living with you.'

'Yes.'

The idea of committing herself to an ongoing relationship with him brought a rush of panic. She wouldn't be free to do what she had to do. 'Adam, I'm booked on a flight to Cambodia tomorrow. The children in the orphanages are expecting me.'

'I wouldn't try to stop your work. I'd support it in every way I could.'

'You don't know...'

'I'll learn.' He released her upper arms and cupped her face, fingers dragging at her skin, reinforcing the urgent intensity in his eyes. 'All the resources at my disposal can be yours, too, Rosalie. Fly on my airline. It won't cost you anything. I'll set up another Saturn company to recruit and pay people who'd like to be involved in your mission. If saving children is your life's work, bring me into it. Share it with me. I'm here for you.'

The bombardment of offers had her mind reeling. 'You haven't thought this through,' she answered weakly.

'I've thought of little else since you left Tortola.'

'It's too much.'

'No. It will never be enough. But together we could make more of a difference, Rosalie.'

Was that true? Or was it all dependent on...his pleasure? 'What if you don't get enough of what you want from me?'

'You think I could cut you off? Cut everything off?' He shook his head, his eyes mocking any possibility of that eventuality. Then he spoke the words she had spoken to him, injecting them with a powerhouse of emotion that ravaged her heart. 'You'll always be part of me. Always. And any part you give me of yourself...it won't be enough...I know it...but it will be better than nothing. And that I also know.'

She wasn't sure. She felt helplessly torn.

'So what I'm offering you now will not be taken away,' he asserted. 'It will not be used as barter for more of your time. It's a gift…in exchange for the gift of having you in my life for at least some of the time.'

Coming home to him…in between trips and modelling assignments…having his support in what she had to do…would it be blind self-indulgence to say *yes?* She wanted to be with him, wanted it so much…but if she gave in to all she felt for him, would she start letting the really important things slide?

'The children have to come first,' she recited frantically. 'They need me.'

'Rosalie…'

Cate's voice, wobbling over her name!

She wrenched herself out of Adam's grasp, instinctively spinning around to deal with the distress she'd heard, alarm beating at her heart over what Adam's daughter might have been listening to, heightening her emotional fragility.

Cate was in the doorway. She wore the same clothes as before—possibly not even having gone to her bedroom to change. Tears were rolling down her cheeks as she shook her head at Rosalie, crying, 'Can't you see?'

Rosalie lifted her hands in automatic appeal for some mutual understanding.

Cate's hands also lifted as she stepped forward, her

whole body leaning into her own appeal. 'Daddy and I…we need you, too,' she choked out, her tear-wet eyes begging for that naked truth to be taken into consideration.

No, it was too much…too much for Rosalie to take on. This was emotional chaos…engulfing her…a net of entrapment closing her into a place that wasn't hers. Cate needed her mother…her mother was gone…it was transference. She had her father. And Adam…he had stood alone before. He could again. There was no *ultimate* need. It wasn't a life and death issue as it was so often with the children. The children…

'I'm sorry…sorry. I can do no more. I have to go.' The words spilled out in taut little jerks. Escape now was paramount. Her heart felt as though it was breaking under the pressure these people were laying on it. 'My bag…' She didn't have it. There, on the sofa. Grab it. Go. Don't look at them again. Don't stop.

'Rosalie…'

Adam calling to her, his deep voice thrumming in her ears, raising goose bumps on her skin, tugging inexorably on the intimate bond that had been forged between them. She'd rushed blindly past Cate, reached the doorway into the front hall, but somehow her feet wouldn't move any further. He was calling to that part of her he owned…that no one else had ever owned.

She looked back.

Anguish in his eyes, burning into her soul.

'Forgive me,' she cried, knowing that his accusation was true.

She *had* started it. Selfishly…wantonly…recklessly…going to Tortola…getting too deeply involved…

He shook his head. 'There's nothing to forgive.'

'Yes, there is,' she replied in an agony of guilt.

But there was no blaming her for anything in his eyes. He looked at her as though he knew everything about her, understood everything about her, and there was not only an absolute acceptance of who she was and what she did but something more, something that caressed and warmed her mangled heart and flowed into the dark places of her soul, making them lighter.

'Nothing to forgive,' he repeated, then softly added, 'I love you.'

CHAPTER FOURTEEN

THEY came...flying in to Tortola from all around the world...every member of the James family. Because it was Rosalie—Rosalie from the Phillipines—who was getting married, and none of them had ever believed she would. They wanted to meet this man who'd won her heart. They wanted to feel sure he was right for her, all that she needed him to be.

It was totally irrelevant that Adam Cazell was a billionaire businessman whose Saturn Companies encompassed global interests. Rosalie was the special one. They knew her as strongly determined, dedicated to her mission, but each and every one of them was aware of her past and the vulnerability of a heart that gave without ever counting the cost to herself. They needed to assure themselves that Adam Cazell was also a giver, not a taker.

Zuang Chi, despite being the star of a much acclaimed operatic tour in Europe, left his role to his understudy. Muhammad and Leah made arrangements for their patients in Calcutta to be cared for by other doctors and nurses. In Hong Kong, Kim set aside the complex legal task of making citizens of refugees. Shasti informed the UNICEF people in Africa she was temporarily needed elsewhere—an important family affair. Zachary Lee, negotiating on a television program in Los Angeles passed the negotiation on to an assistant.

In Australia, Joel Faber, Tiffany Makana's husband, organised the travel arrangements for those of the family living there, also ensuring that Carol and Alan Tay's tourism business in Haven Bay would be looked after while they were away. Suzanne Griffith and her husband, Leith Carew, flew from the Barossa Valley in South Australia, leaving their vineyards in the able hands of Leith's father and collecting Tom from Alice Springs on their way to Brisbane to join the others for the big trip.

Joseph, in Thailand, promised the orphans in his school lots of photographs of Rosalie's wedding and used the special ticket Adam Cazell had sent him to fly free on any Saturn plane. Breaking their tour of South America, Edward and Hilary James, who had gathered so many lost children into a family, made their own way to Tortola to see their adopted daughter married... Rosalie, at last finding the love *she* most needed...they hoped.

Rebel and Hugh brought Celeste with them—still Cate's best friend—and were special guests at Adam's villa on Tortola. Rebel was to be Rosalie's matron of honour at the wedding, Hugh, Adam's best man. It was at Davenport Hall, on Christmas Eve, that this marriage had been proposed and agreed to. Neither of them had any doubts that a pledge based on a very special love had been made.

Nevertheless, Rebel understood that the family would have to see it for themselves.

Rosalie was…Rosalie.

So they all came to Tortola, arriving on many different flights. Transport was waiting for them. Private villas had been rented to accommodate them, people employed to see to their every need. Adam was as keen to meet the remarkable James family as they were to meet him, curious to see the influence of their supportive network in play. He held open house at his villa for any one or all of them to drop in whenever they wanted to, prior to the big day of the wedding.

Celeste had told Cate the stories behind each adoption into the family, actually going so far as to advise her, 'You should get Rosalie to adopt you, like Rebel did me. Then legally you're one of them, too. You'll want to be once you meet them. The whole family is amazing!'

Cate was over the moon anyway, so delighted that Rosalie was going to marry her father that it wouldn't have mattered what the James family was like, but she was intrigued and impressed by them; Leah so graceful and feminine in her beautiful saris, Shasti stunningly regal wearing a turban and Ethiopian robes, Tom, the aboriginal Australian, with all the dignity of his ancient race.

Adam was very conscious of them making their assessment of him and how he behaved towards their sister. Their observation was subtle. So was the probing about future plans. It felt like fine tentacles of caring weaving through everything they said, touching lightly on him, more sensing for truth than testing for it. Gradually what reservations they'd held gave way to warm approval and Adam felt himself being drawn into what he thought of as their charmed circle, a place where what they were all about was understood as right for each person.

'How was it for you when you met them?' he asked Hugh when they had some time alone together.

They were sitting on the verandah overlooking the cove, enjoying the sea breeze and a relaxing drink. Most of the family had left after a very long luncheon. Rebel was going over tomorrow's wedding ceremony with Edward and Hilary. Cate and Celeste had raced off for a swim. Rosalie was strolling along the beach with Zachary Lee, the big brother who had once incited intense jealousy in Adam, but who now had his deepest gratitude for having saved Rosalie.

Hugh slanted him a sympathetic smile. 'Overwhelming, at first. They're such positive people. It's like…nothing can defeat them. They made me feel ashamed of what I'd been and determined to become a better man.' He heaved a rueful sigh, then added, 'But most of all I felt privileged that Rebel had chosen to marry me.'

Privileged…yes. Adam nodded. 'We're both very fortunate men, Hugh.'

'You have the harder road with Rosalie. Rebel was content to make her home with me.'

'We don't have to be in the one place. That's not

how it is for us. It's knowing we can come home to each other. Always.'

Hugh looked somewhat bemused. 'That's almost exactly what Rebel said. Right from the time she saw the two of you together at Davenport Hall, she figured if there was any man for Rosalie, you were it. That's why she gave you the Mayfair telephone number.'

'Is that so?' Adam grinned, recalling how he thought he'd manipulated Rebel into giving it. 'Smart woman, your wife.'

'Mmmh...used to be a super sales person. Did her best to sell you to Rosalie, too, but she honestly thought the fortress gates had remained shut. Came as a big surprise when she found out Rosalie had opened them to you.'

*The fortress gates...*it was an evocative phrase.

She had let him in. But it was only love that kept the gates open, that made her feel safe with him. Adam silently vowed he would never give her reason to doubt his love, that it would be reaffirmed whenever he saw the slightest need in her to have it reaffirmed. He wanted Rosalie to feel safe with him for the rest of their lives.

They walked along the water's edge where the sand was firm, their bare feet catching the occasional swirl of froth from the gentle waves. Of all her brothers and sisters, Rosalie was most comfortable with Zachary Lee. She'd trusted him before she'd trusted anyone else.

'This is a beautiful place,' he remarked appreciatively.

'Yes. It's where I first came to know and trust Adam.'

'Were you frightened?'

'Yes and no. I felt...a compulsion...to be with him like that...even though the idea was scary. Then I just wanted him more and more. He made me feel safe with him, Zachary.'

'Yes. I can see that is so.'

They smiled at each other, their understanding encompassing more than could be put into words.

'Adam is like you in a lot of ways. Big...'

Laughter bubbled up from his huge barrel chest. His eyes merrily teased her. 'I didn't know you'd peeked at me in the raw.'

She thumped him, then laughed as heat rushed into her cheeks. 'I meant big in his mind and heart. But I have to admit I love his body, too.'

'Good!' His eyes softened as he added, 'Then your world is now in better balance, Rosalie. As all of us have wanted it to be for you.'

She frowned. 'Was I so wrong, Zachary?'

'No. Not wrong. Just...incomplete. And now Adam fills the place you'd blanked out of your life.'

Blanked out...the realisation dawned on her that she had done precisely that—put up a barrier that precluded any man from getting close to her, denying that the woman inside her had any use for one.

Until Adam, who'd stirred both need and desire,

awakening the woman she'd blanked out, giving her his love.

Asking nothing.

Just giving.

Giving as she had given hundreds of times to children who had *blanked out*, because it was needed, and only when Adam gave her his love had she known that she needed it, too…needed it from him.

A big man…as big as her dearest brother, Zachary Lee, who had rescued her. Adam had rescued her, too. From the loneliness she had thought was an inevitable outcome from the path she had chosen. But it wasn't so. Adam had shown her how it could be. How it was now. Together. Sharing everything.

Except…she suddenly thought of something else she'd blanked out of her life—something Adam had asked her about on their first night here. A child of her own. She'd denied any possibility of it, but now…not a child of her own but one created from their love for each other. His child, too.

She smiled.

Continuance.

As Rebel said, passing on the love to help make the world a better place.

'Is that a private smile or one you can share?' Zachary Lee asked teasingly.

She grinned happily at him. 'This one belongs to Adam. I'll share it with him tonight.'

'The wedding is not until tomorrow,' came the arch reminder.

She laughed. 'Adam wanted to have it made legal. As his wife I'd always have direct access to anything he owned. He wanted me to feel secure about that. But the bond between us…it doesn't need any reinforcement, Zachary.'

'So we're just celebrating it, are we?'

'Yes.'

'Well, it gives us the chance to feel happy for you. And we are, Rosalie. All of us.'

It was a glorious morning. Perfect, Adam thought. Nature at its best. A more fitting showcase for the bride of his heart than any cathedral in the world. Which she could have had if she'd wanted it, along with a designer wedding dress dripping with diamonds. But such things didn't matter to Rosalie. She'd wanted to be married here, on the island, out in the open and with only the family present.

No formal clothes. Most of the men were dressed in similar clothes to himself and Hugh—brightly patterned, open-necked, floral shirts and white trousers. The women were just as colourful, told to wear whatever they pleased and felt comfortable in. He'd seen Cate and Celeste in matching turquoise sarongs, dashing around to get *their* music set up for the wedding.

'Does Rosalie know about this?' he'd asked.

'It's a surprise, Dad,' Cate had declared excitedly.

'And absolutely right,' Celeste had assured him.

It was time now. The family had gathered under the shade of a big mango tree. A local wedding celebrant was waiting beside Adam and Hugh. Cate and Celeste had taken up a poised position on the edge of the verandah, both of them carrying baskets.

The hi-fi speakers they'd set up suddenly burst into sound. It was an old Abba song—*Take a Chance On Me*—and the two girls danced off the verandah steps and literally bopped down the makeshift aisle to the cheerful beat of the music, happily hurling flower petals from their baskets in all directions. Their exuberance made everyone smile. And Rebel, trailing after them in a royal blue sarong and with a huge grin on her face, wasn't above doing a few joyful dance steps herself.

Chances indeed taken, Adam thought, and here they were, celebrating the outcome.

The music ended. The girls joined the family gathering. Rebel took her place near the marriage celebrant. All heads were turned to the verandah as Rosalie made her appearance, flanked by Edward—the only father she'd known—and Zuang Chi, who had offered to sing a song for his sister and the man she'd chosen to marry.

Adam felt his heart swell at this first sight of his bride. He'd seen her in many roles, dressed like a queen or with the simplicity of a peasant. Today she looked as ethereal as a vestal virgin and as earthy as an island princess, incredibly beautiful, and glowing with an incandescent smile aimed straight at him.

She wore a filmy white sarong tied over one shoulder. Her long glorious hair swept down over the other shoulder, falling to her waist. A garland of frangipani flowers circled her head. She carried a spray of them in one hand. As she stepped off the verandah, the rippling drape of the sarong parted to show bare legs, and he saw that her feet were bare, too.

As though she was coming to him with nothing but herself.

It was more than enough for Adam.

This woman, whom he cherished beyond anything he'd ever held dear, was about to become his wife.

Rosalie felt Adam's love pouring out to her as she walked towards him. Behind her, she heard Zuang Chi's magnificent voice lift into the song, *There for me,* and she knew it was true of Adam. She hoped he knew it was true of her, too, that she would always do her best to answer his needs.

They did belong together. She was certain of it now. Adam...the first man...the only man for her...mind, heart and soul reaching out...mating forever.

He held out his hand to her.

She placed hers into it, knowing she was safe with him.

Always.

She looked into his eyes, and the need to say the words that expressed all she felt for him welled up and spilled from her lips...

'I love you.'

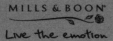

MILLS & BOON®

Live the emotion

Modern Romance™

THE SALVATORE MARRIAGE by *Michelle Reid*

A tragic accident reunites Shannon Gilbraith with Luca Salvatore. But Shannon isn't prepared for the instant attraction that re-ignites between them. Luca presses Shannon to marry him; she knows it's only for the sake of her tiny orphaned niece – but what does the future hold...?

THE CHRISTMAS MARRIAGE MISSION by *Helen Brooks*

When Kay Sherwood cruises into Mitchell Grey's office he's so fiercely attracted to her he insists she join him for dinner. Mitchell indulges in no-strings affairs – getting intimate with Kay would be dangerous. But he hasn't counted on some special seasonal magic...

THE SPANIARD'S PASSION by *Jane Porter*

Sophie can never forget that she only agreed to her loveless marriage to escape her overwhelming attraction for another man – South American millionaire Alonso Galván. Now penniless, the only way to put the past behind her is to travel to South America...

THE YULETIDE ENGAGEMENT by *Carole Mortimer*

Pride stops Ellie Fairfax from asking sexy Patrick McGrath to accompany her to her boss's Christmas party. Patrick wants Ellie, but is worried she might be pining for her devious ex-boyfriend. As for Ellie – she just wants to show Patrick that he's top of her Christmas wish-list!

On sale 5th December 2003

Available at most branches of WHSmith, Tesco, Martins, Borders, Eason, Sainsbury's and all good paperback bookshops.

1103/01a

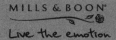

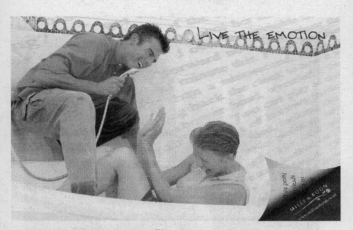

LIVE THE EMOTION

Modern Romance™
...seduction and
passion guaranteed

Tender Romance™
...love affairs that
last a lifetime

Medical Romance™
...medical drama
on the pulse

Historical Romance™
...rich, vivid and
passionate

Sensual Romance™
...sassy, sexy and
seductive

Blaze Romance™
...the temperature's
rising

27 new titles every month.

Live the emotion

MILLS & BOON®

MILLS & BOON®

BETTY NEELS

THE CHRISTMAS COLLECTION

On sale 5th December 2003

Available at most branches of WH Smith, Tesco, Martins, Borders, Eason, Sainsbury's and all good paperback bookshops.

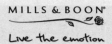

FREE!

4 Books
and a surprise gift!

We would like to take this opportunity to thank you for reading this Mills & Boon® book by offering you the chance to take FOUR more specially selected titles from the Modern Romance™ series absolutely FREE! We're also making this offer to introduce you to the benefits of the Reader Service™—

- ★ FREE home delivery
- ★ FREE gifts and competitions
- ★ FREE monthly Newsletter
- ★ Books available before they're in the shops
- ★ Exclusive Reader Service discount

Accepting these FREE books and gift places you under no obligation to buy; you may cancel at any time, even after receiving your free shipment. Simply complete your details below and return the entire page to the address below. *You don't even need a stamp!*

YES! Please send me 4 free Modern Romance books and a surprise gift. I understand that unless you hear from me, I will receive 6 superb new titles every month for just £2.60 each, postage and packing free. I am under no obligation to purchase any books and may cancel my subscription at any time. The free books and gift will be mine to keep in any case.

P3ZEF

Ms/Mrs/Miss/Mr ....Initials...
BLOCK CAPITALS PLEASE

Surname...

Address...

....

....Postcode ....

Send this whole page to:
UK: The Reader Service, FREEPOST CN81, Croydon, CR9 3WZ
EIRE: The Reader Service, PO Box 4546, Kilcock, County Kildare (stamp required)